DARK AND BROKEN THINGS

a novel by

John Mulhall

1st Edition. Printed in the United States of America.

Published by Blanket Fort Books

Softcover ISBN: 978-0-9885949-5-1
Hardcover ISBN: 978-0-9885949-6-8
Audiobook ISBN: 978-0-9885949-7-5

www.darkandbrokenthings.com
www.johnmulhall.com
www.facebook.com/authorjohnmulhall

Cover Art by Scott Zambelli
Dark and Broken Things Logo and Cover Layout by Grant England
Layout by Natalie DeSavia
Author Photo by Moses Sparks Photography, mosessparks.com
Developmental Editing by Naz Keynejad
Copy Editing by Linda Daft Larsen and Terrie Mathis

For Linda Larsen, for believing in me,
and investing so much of your time and energy
in order to make sure that others saw what you saw.

And also for providing a bit of inspiration for this story.

"If you seek the kernel, then you must break the shell. And likewise, if you would know the reality of Nature, you must destroy the appearance, and the farther you go beyond the appearance, the nearer you will be to the essence."

- Meister Eckhart

PART I:
THE ACCIDENT

THE ACCIDENT

1

The tires squealed in the snow.

At least he thought that's what the noise was.

It was either that or the shriek of the metal guardrail. The wail of the trees as they bent sideways, scraping down the sides of the Jeep.

Maybe it wasn't the tires at all.

He wondered if they were even touching the ground anymore. He wondered why he had the time to be wondering anything. It all seemed to be happening in slow motion, as if it were happening to someone else. As if it weren't even real.

His hands on the steering wheel felt numb.

He felt the vehicle list to the side and became vaguely aware of the seatbelt cutting into his neck. His eyes drifted languidly to the rearview mirror, and he caught a fleeting glimpse of his own unshaven face, dispassionate, his dark hair standing straight up, defying gravity.

Not thirty seconds earlier, everything had been normal. His friend James had made a dismissive comment about The White Stripes, and he had been quick to defend them, reaching for the coffee mug nestled solidly in the center console.

Thirty seconds ago…five minutes…a lifetime…

The scenery in front of the Jeep shifted, an impressionist painting of pine and snow. The windshield cracked. And he suddenly became aware of James screaming.

He wished they could go back to joking about the little things. He wished this were still a friendly road trip. What he wouldn't give to go back.

He heard the sound of metal bending. Felt the compartment of the Jeep shifting around them. Tasted blood in his mouth.

The White Stripes, he thought, *are a fantastic fucking rock band.*

2

A moment of bright white – the sun reflecting off the snow perhaps, intruding on the compartment of the Jeep – and then darkness.

He could hear the sound of the vehicle settling, rocking in place, the sound of air escaping from…somewhere. And then, there was something else. Faint. Like the sound of a bird somewhere in the distance, chirping repeatedly. Rhythmically. Musically.

It was *familiar*.

He found the darkness agreeable, comforting, like a warm blanket. But a part of him deep inside, a hidden voice, urged him to open his eyes, to check on James. There was work to do.

But the darkness was pleasant.

The bird continued. Up the scale, and then again. Three notes. Up the scale, and then again. Like a soothing lullaby.

Open your eyes, David.

It was his father's voice.

Open your eyes, David. We're Graces. We don't quit.

A memory of his father. It was jarring. He hadn't thought of the man in a long time. Now, suddenly, here he was. And David was ten-years-old again. His father, dressed in a blue button-up dress shirt – meticulously ironed, the collar perfectly starched and rigid – was sitting on the edge of David's bed. It had been a long time since he'd seen his father and he'd almost forgotten how penetrating his blue eyes could be, almost forgotten how manicured his appearance had been, how short and precise his haircut. David smelled the hint of cigarettes: Marlboro Lights.

In this memory, his father's hand was on his shoulder. But that wasn't accurate, was it? No. His father had rarely touched him.

We're Graces. And life must go on. We don't quit. Now get up, and get dressed.

David struggled to open his eyes, like a good soldier.

But the darkness – so agreeable!

His eyelids fluttered and a blade of vivid white pierced the veil. And then there was something else. Something dark. Red. Heavy. It was clouding his vision, sticking to his eyelashes. Blood. There was blood in his eyes. Strange. He didn't feel injured at all. Just comfortable. He blinked as if he could dismiss the liquid like the remnants of a deep sleep.

He became aware, quite suddenly, that it was cold. His stomach, his arms; they were freezing. He was lying in the snow, on the ice. His heavy jacket hadn't been needed in the warmth of the Jeep, not with its hardcover top latched down and the heater going full blast. David was lying in the snow in his shirtsleeves.

"They're overrated," James had said not long before, casually dismissing one of David's favorite bands as The White Stripes' "You're Pretty Good Looking" began to play on David's iPod. James' voice crept back into David's mind now. "They're a garage band that got lucky. Right place, right time."

Heresy.

Where was he? Where was James now? David blinked again, trying to focus. He attempted to lift his head, but his entire body felt heavy. Almost impossibly so.

The darkness is sooooo nice. Just enjoy it a few minutes longer.

He opened and closed his eyes a few more times. He tried to move, but it was too much effort. His vision suddenly came into a tenuous sort of focus, and as he blinked, he could make out blurry images, his brain taking them in like snapshots from an old camera: the Jeep, what was left of it, at an odd angle, nearby; a tire spinning absently, like a pinwheel, winding down under its own momentum; the dripping of fluids, blue and tan, from the upturned underbelly of the vehicle; James, his head resting against the snow, his eyes wide open, his face torn down the center in a vertical gash that started at his forehead, moved between his eyes, split his nose and lips through the middle, and ended at his chin.

David felt a twinge move through him, and he closed his eyes again.

Just a few more minutes.

It was safe in the darkness.

And the bird was back. Up the scale, and then again. Three notes. Up the scale, and then again.

A lullaby.

3

Three notes in quick succession. After a moment, he thought he recognized the pattern the bird was chirping.

G#, C#, E. – G#, C#, E. – G#, C#, E.

And then a change. So familiar.

No wait, not a bird at all. He knew this. It was the tinkling of a piano. With him at the keyboard. At ten, maybe eleven years old.

No, it was ten. It was ten, for sure.

G#, C#, E – G#, C#, E – G#, C#, E

A, C#, E – A, D, F# - G#, C, F#

Ah! He knew this!

"Moonlight Sonata." Beethoven.

How many times had he sat there at that old piano while his friends had been outside at play and repeated those same notes? In the dusty file cabinet of his memory, this one had been filed deep. He at the keyboard, his father hovering, perhaps preparing dinner, and his mother placed at the window in her wheelchair.

Yes, he had been ten for sure.

The music from David practicing the piano had formed a sort of underlying soundtrack to their lives during that period of time, something he only realized in retrospect. So many repeated notes. So much time spent practicing.

But David hadn't touched a piano now in almost twenty years.

The music continued and he relaxed, allowing it to pull him further into the dark.

4

It was the first time he'd felt this relaxed, this *safe*, in a long, long while. He allowed himself to ease into it, this darkness, like one eases oneself into a warm bath. Perhaps it'll be too hot? Not quite warm enough? *No, perfect.* Aches and pains can be forgotten momentarily.

His brain seemed to loosen inside his skull, and float away. He imagined it disintegrating, piece by piece, atom by atom, moving out across the outer darkness, spreading itself so thin that it was no longer visible anymore. Still there, but improved, a part of something larger. He imagined it as a beautiful sandcastle, once meticulously crafted by tiny hands, now slowly eroding away, simply becoming part of the beach again.

He wanted it. He was ready.

Open your eyes, David. We're Graces. We don't quit!

CLEAR!

He felt his body spasm.

5

The voices seemed to come from afar at first, tiny intrusions on his peace, like flies buzzing. Buzzing around his head. Invading his picnic.

CLEAR!

Another spasm.

He felt himself being pulled up, away from the outer darkness, from the pleasantness. And he began to feel the cold again. An aching down his right side. His leg, his arm. Tingling.

I've got a rhythm.

The bright light had returned. No, it wasn't the same. Not the glare from the snow, but rather the light from a miniature flashlight. Floating. Invasive.

Buzz, buzz.

Just a few more minutes, Dad.

Another series of snapshots before his eyes closed again: a room with dingy green walls; a man in blue surgical scrubs looming over him, waving the tiny light in front of his eyes, besetting his peace; a machine counting the beats of his heart.

David realized that the beeping of the machine synched perfectly with "Moonlight Sonata."

Had that still been playing? Even in the darkness? Still?

For a brief moment, he saw an image of his mother as she was before her accident. Before the wheelchair. Long dirty-blonde hair, gentle features. She was smiling at him, her hand on his face, under his chin. Her eyes were kind. He didn't have many memories like this anymore, of her looking vibrant, strong, human. Just old pictures, mostly forgotten, mostly misplaced.

David, she whispered.

His name's David...

David, you're a crazy child, and I love you.

...unresponsive...

He felt himself drifting away again, being pulled, not to the same pleasing darkness, the same warm, welcoming abyss, but under waves of gray murk. His blood felt warm in his veins. Was he drowning? Was there something in his throat?

...operate...

He could feel his heart beating. It was shallow, slow, but it was there.

David, darling, you know you can't have Apple Jacks for dinner. What would your father say?

...bone saw...

The machine continued to act as a steady metronome, counting off beats, beeping in time to the minor progression of the song in his mind.

6

"Elbows off the table," his father said. There was no sternness to his voice. There was little color to his voice at all. It was rote.

David longed for color.

It was just after his mother's accident. The house was quiet. And color had all but gone out of his world.

David and his father ate across from each other, but didn't speak much. His father made vague attempts at communication – *How was your day at school?* – but he merely listened to David's responses, nodded perfunctorily, and never followed up.

Make conversation with son. Check.

After dinner, his father asked him, as was becoming usual, to move his mother by the window. His father felt that she liked the window and the view. They lived on the second floor of a duplex in Sherman Oaks, California, and the front window faced the street. It presented a view of the trees in the yard, the flower beds, the street beyond, the neighborhood at rest and at play. And at night, the stars and sometimes the moon. In addition, an open window in August offered a pleasant and welcome breeze.

"Daaviiid," she moaned, as he approached her ensconced form. "Daaaaaviid."

He was ten. And his mother had become a monster to him, trapped in steel, her face drooping on one side, her speech minimal at best, incoherent and seemingly angry at worst. Even on her best days, she was just barely able to move the giant wheels on the chair by herself.

Her head bobbed in a slight, lizard-like manner. And David watched the spittle trickle down her chin.

This wasn't his mother. Wasn't the same person who'd picked him up, carried him, loved him. Who'd gazed into his face. Radiated warmth. Made him feel safe. A man in a car had taken *that* woman away, and left in her place, lying helplessly in the middle of an empty street, bent and bleeding, *this*.

"Daaaaaaviid," she moaned, her head lolling to the side, toward him. He recoiled involuntarily. He knew that he shouldn't. This was still his mother. That's what they'd all promised him. The doctors. The experts. Traumatic brain injury, they'd said.

Traumatic.

He rolled her over to the window as his father had requested. The large wheels on the wheelchair spun slowly, squeaking faintly as they turned, the floorboards creaking under their weight.

He locked the wheels down and moved away from her.

"Daavid," she groaned.

There was a part of him that knew she wanted him to stay with her, that knew that she was trying to communicate. But he couldn't. He couldn't look at her. She wasn't his mother.

He just couldn't.

7

He's waking up.

His head felt sluggish. Where was he again? The ski trip. With James. Their annual ski trip. They'd been coming home. Yes, right, that's right. The accident. An innocent reach for a sip of coffee. Wheels catching black ice. A slight wobble of the steering wheel, just enough. And now a green room, men and women in blue scrubs, and the mingling smells of antiseptic and…something else, something burning.

It was hard to focus. He felt that drowning sensation again. He tried to lift his head.

I got him. Upping the anesthesia.

A nurse moved to him. She was short, full. Her dark eyes peered out from under the blue surgical cap. Her other features were obscured by a mask.

"David, we need you to lie back, okay?"

She pushed gently on his chest. He reached up with his left hand to touch his face, but she deflected it. Where was his right hand? Restrained?

"You're intubated. You've got a tube in your throat to help you breathe, okay?" She spoke slowly, punching each syllable. "You need to leave it there. Just close your eyes."

He felt his head getting fuzzy again.

And he thought of James, lying in the snow, eyes locked open. He thought of the wheel of the Jeep, slowly spinning.

No, that was wrong. It was the wheel of a wheelchair. It was the wheel of a wheelchair upended, turning sluggishly, clicking like a pinwheel.

No.

THE ACCIDENT

No, it was the Jeep. They'd had an accident. He could practically feel the snow on his belly. Cold. He was cold.

And then he sank back beneath the murky waves.

8

"You stay in here. You'll have plenty of time to think about what you've done," his father said, slamming the door of David's tiny room. The noise echoed in David's ears.

He was thirteen now.

Thirteen. And he'd taken a gun to school.

David had often fantasized about them finding the man who'd taken his mother from him. He just *assumed* it was a man – he didn't know why, exactly. He'd often wondered what the man would look like. In his mind's eye, David had pictured him as being a short man with a wide nose, scruffy hair, and deeply set eyes. The man had a broad neck and spoke with an accent; David wasn't sure exactly what kind of accent it was though. The man had been wearing a suit; he'd been wearing a suit on the witness stand in front of a jury. And he'd been overwhelmingly convicted.

But that wasn't the truth. They'd never found anyone. Except his mother, prostrate on the road, bleeding from the head. They didn't even know how long she'd been there.

Now, less than three years later, she was gone.

Maybe the accident hadn't killed her, maybe not directly. But David knew without a doubt that the man driving was responsible. A man had destroyed their lives. And then simply kept driving.

Lately, David had become obsessed with the idea of finding him. Tracking him down like Remington Steele or Thomas Magnum. Because that's how things were supposed to end. The bad guy gets his. Justice is served. Roll credits.

But life didn't seem to be working out that way.

Often, David would close his eyes and picture this fictitious man on his knees begging for David's mercy: "I didn't mean to hit her. I'm sorry I just kept driving! I didn't mean to hit her! I'm sorry I just kept driving!" David would imagine the man begging, and David would pull the trigger anyway. He'd imagine how loud the gunshot would be. How satisfied he'd feel. Getting revenge, finally, for his mother, for his family, and for himself. The cathartic fantasy of a child who was now moving into young adulthood.

The gun David had taken to school belonged to his father. As an ex-Army man and a hunter, his father had always kept firearms around the house. But he'd also always instructed David in their use, allowed David to watch as he'd cleaned them, and even took David shooting a couple of times. He'd taught respect for firearms.

The gun was a Beretta Model 1934. It had originally belonged to his grandfather, who'd gotten it during World War II. David had appropriated the gun from his father's nightstand. It was unloaded and locked.

Plenty of time to think about what you've done.

But what had he done? Taken the gun to school, yes. That's what. It would've been better if his father had asked him to think about *why*. *That* was the riddle. That was the question that would've tormented him. Because he simply didn't know. He didn't know why he did a lot of the things he did these days. He just knew that he was angry *all the time now*, and desperately searching for some way not to be. He knew that the gun in his hand had made him feel in control, ever so briefly. He knew that he'd enjoyed showing it to his friends, seeing the admiration in their young eyes. He knew that much.

When his father returned later that evening, David was still sitting in the same position on the bed. Still staring at the same wall. His father sat next to him and looked at him intently. "Well? Are you ready to tell me?"

David thought for a moment before answering the unanswerable. Finally, he shook his head and said quietly, "I hate him."

His father didn't ask whom David meant. He simply nodded.

"David," he sighed. "I know you think that finding that man, punishing him, would make you feel better. But son, you're wrong. You'll realize that someday, I promise. If you were to use that gun on another man, it would wound you both. Forever."

David didn't really know what his father had meant by that. He knew that his father was reaching out in a way he rarely tried, and still, David couldn't help but resent the *timing* of the lecture.

"We become what we can't forgive, David. I don't want that for you."

His father rose and walked to the door. He turned back around and looked at David, sighing deeply. There was more to say. Both of them knew it. There were words that would never be uttered.

"There's dinner for you downstairs. If you want some."

9

The memory of his father faded away and David's eyes fluttered.

He found himself drifting languidly down a long hallway lit from above by fluorescent lights, which made yellow walls appear sickly. In the background, he could hear the squeaking of small wheels on tile. The beeping of machines. *"Moonlight Sonata."*

As he watched the ceiling drift by, the overhead lights flickered and dropped out, and then the lighting changed; different fluorescents kicked in at the sides of the hall, dimmer lights, which had no less tainting an effect on the walls. People passed by as he glided down the corridor, phantoms skating along the edge of his vision.

David's body ached. His right side more than the rest.

Was there still something in his throat?

For a moment, the squeaking of the gurney wheels sounded an awful lot like the turning of his mother's wheelchair and he felt his heart jump at the notion. *Silly, silly thoughts.*

At the end of the hallway was a dark room. Or was it just darkness? Was it just that amazing infinite darkness that had felt so comfortable before? A part of him hoped that it was.

His body floated along toward it.

Was someone laughing? Were those footsteps? So much ambient noise here now, creeping in. He tried to hum along to "Moonlight Sonata," but it came out as nothing more than a groan.

"Just one minute, Mr. Grace, we're almost there. We'll get that taken care of."

As his body glided down the hallway, supported only by the tenuous, quavering wheels on the gurney, David tilted his head sluggishly to the side and saw a woman standing in the darkness of the hallway, watching him go by. An old woman with a kind face, dressed in black. She was there a moment, smiling at him and then the gurney was pushing on, past her, toward the darkness.

No, not darkness. Just a room. Getting closer.

David closed his eyes again.

PART II:
VISITING HOURS

10

It was daytime. He could tell that much, even though the windows of his small hospital room had been boarded up from the outside.

His eyes moved around the room: the walls were the same sickly yellow color he remembered vaguely from his trip down the long hallway; there was another bed next to him on the left, empty; his right arm was in bandages; a woman who looked to him to be of Indian ethnicity – a nurse…no, most likely a doctor – was scribbling on a clipboard; a wheelchair was placed diagonally near the end of his bed.

The woman noticed him stirring, stopped writing, and moved to him, holding the clipboard at her side. "Hi there, David. How are you feeling this morning?"

David swallowed hard before speaking and then said, "My…throat…hurts."

"Yes, that's normal. You were intubated. But it should go away in a little bit. Drink a little bit of water, not too much. And chew on ice chips."

"Okay."

"I'm Dr. Devar." She was attractive, demure, with eyes like saucers, and fine, straight, shoulder-length black hair. "I operated on you when you were brought in yesterday. What do you remember?"

The darkness.

"Um, I remember…"

Bone saw.

"…I remember driving home with my friend James after our ski trip…"

The White Stripes.

He paused.

"Is that all?" she asked, narrowing her eyes.

Think about what you've done.

He nodded. "It's all…jumbled." A pause and then, "We had an accident, didn't we?"

"Yes. I'm afraid you did. Your car went off the side of an embankment into the snow. You were…very lucky to be found, actually."

"James?"

The softness of her features transitioned into solemnity. David knew the look very well. He had seen this face too many times in his life. The first time had also been in a hospital. Devar was a doctor; that meant she had become proficient at delivering bad news.

She shook her head. "I'm sorry."

"Oh…god…"

"Your friend died instantly in the crash. There was nothing anyone could do."

David felt the tears sting his weary eyes, but he pushed them away. The image of James – him lying with his face in the snow, his neck twisted awkwardly – flashed into his mind.

"David," Dr. Devar said carefully, "there's something else you need to know."

David looked up at her face; she wasn't done delivering bad news.

"What…what else?"

"You nearly died in that crash as well. Your vehicle rolled and your right arm and right leg were trapped underneath. Your arm was cut and badly bruised, but we think it will be all right. Your leg, however, was…it was crushed, David. I'm very sorry to say that we tried, but we weren't able to save it."

He felt that he must have heard her wrong. Couldn't save...*what?* His leg? His leg was right there under the blankets. He could feel...

David looked down at the covers and froze. There was a discernible lack of mass where his right leg should be. Past the knee, the covers just fell away. He felt dizzy suddenly, nauseated. He was seized by fear and a peculiar sense of loneliness, but the fear quickly gave way to a swelling anger.

"I'm very sorry," Dr. Devar said. "I know how shocking this all must be. But believe me when I tell you that you're very lucky just to be alive. Often in accidents like this..."

"You took my fucking leg?!"

Dr. Devar seemed taken aback by the suddenness of David's outburst but not by the reaction itself. She took a breath, waited a moment, and then replied, "I'm very sorry, but it was a life threatening injury and it had to be done. I promise you that."

David wanted to scream. So many thoughts, so many feelings were flooding through him all at once. Processing the loss of James was overwhelming enough, but this? He couldn't even begin. He just wanted to be back in the Jeep, pushing on the gas, making jokes with his best friend, and heading home. He wanted to be skiing.

He'd miss skiing.

He was incomplete.

He missed the darkness then; he longed for it.

David realized that the doctor was still speaking although he hadn't heard most of what she'd said: "...remarkable things that they can do these days in the world of prosthetic devices. I'd be happy to talk about your options when you..."

"Please!" David snapped. "Please, just...just, give me a moment."

Dr. Devar nodded. "Absolutely. Take your time. I'm just down the hall if you need me. Just hit the call button any time. I put a wheelchair here for you, in case…."

"No," he said curtly.

"I'm sorry?"

"Get it out of here!" he barked.

"I don't under…"

"That! That thing. I have a… I just don't want it in here! Get it out of here!" His mind was racing. His pulse had quickened. He wanted to run far away but had to stifle a bitter laugh at the irony of the thought. He was suddenly pissed at James for even talking about The White Stripes. *That* had been the start of all of this.

Dr. Devar pulled the wheelchair away from his bed and rolled it toward the door. "It's going to be okay, David. Take your time. I'll be here when you're ready to talk."

The rubber on the wheelchair's tires screeched against the tile floor as she rolled it out of view.

11

The overhead fluorescent lights blinked and then went out. They were immediately replaced by the safety lighting at the sides of the room. David couldn't help but feel like he was trapped in a submarine.

The nurse came in, moving briskly. She was a zaftig woman, striking in a deconstructed way: her long hair was pulled back into a simple ponytail, her face was bereft of all traces of makeup, her yellow patterned scrubs were stained. Her name was Monica, if he recalled. Or perhaps it was Monique. She'd been in several times to change his bandages, adjust his medicine, and bring him his meals.

"You're not gonna eat your food?" she asked, barely glancing at the untouched plate in front of him. She lifted his chart from the hook on the wall near the bed and made a quick notation, then moved to his IV and adjusted it.

Upping his painkillers, he hoped.

"You've got to eat, you know," she said.

"Why are the lights doing this?"

She looked around the room, almost as if she hadn't noticed. "We're on generator power, hon. Didn't the doctor talk to you about the state of the hospital?"

He moved his head back and forth. It was the least possible amount of effort he could make and still have her understand that he was saying *no.*

"There's a blizzard. A *bad* one. You're lucky they got you here before it hit us."

He knew about the storm moving in. It was the reason the ski resort had shut down. The reason he and James had started home early.

"*And* you're lucky we were still open," she continued. "We typically evacuate if the storms get too bad up here. But this one came on too fast. So we're all stuck here together, at least until the storm passes. One big happy family." She smiled.

Stuck here. That was an understatement.

He turned his head to the window. Very little daylight peeked through now, from behind the boards and the curtains. It was still daytime though. He could feel it.

"What can I do to get you to eat?" the nurse asked.

He didn't respond.

"David?"

"I'll eat when I'm hungry."

"Yeah, but see…we really need you to eat. You've had a lot of medication in you, and a surgery, and we need to make sure your body's getting…"

"I'll eat when I'm fucking hungry," he spat.

She raised an eyebrow.

He knew she was just doing her job, but he didn't care. He really just wanted her to go away.

"Alright then," she said, and began to leave. "It'll be time for your physical therapy soon though, hon. And he's not as forgiving as I am."

David closed his eyes and waited for the medication to kick in.

12

"She's a smokin' hottie," James said. "You're nuts if you skip out on that."

It was James, sitting next to him on a ski lift as they rode up the mountain, wiping his goggles clean.

When was this? David wondered. *Just a week ago? Before the accident?*

No.

No, it was several years before. Memories of their annual ski trips had come to blend together in the best possible way, a fusion of disparate good times and debauchery, coated in a hazy sheen of cocktails.

It was James, it was several years before, and he was talking about Dana.

"One smokin' hottie versus a whole wide world full of smokin' hotties?" David asked flippantly. "And two things, by the way: when did we start using the term 'smokin hotties,' and when the hell did you get so sentimental about this girl?"

James spit into his goggles and scrubbed with the fingertips of his gloves. He shook his head. "I don't know, I guess I'm getting soft in my old age. I like her though. She's better than you deserve."

"Gee, thanks, buddy," David laughed.

"No problem, pal. Except for the whole David-Dana thing. David-Dana, David-Dana. A little too…what do you call it?"

"Alliterative?"

"No," James said, "that is *definitely* not the word I was thinking of. What does that even mean?"

"It means the words start with the same sound."

"Oh. Well then, yeah, that's the word. I kinda hate that stuff, but I'll make an exception this time as long as you don't name your kids Darryl, Dane, and Danny. Notice: all boys."

"No kids. But it doesn't matter anyway. I'm breaking it off with her. I've just got to find the right time," David said.

"Fine." James sighed. "Damn it, I really liked those little breakfast things she made…the little thin pancake-y things?"

"Crepes?"

"Yes! Those. Yum."

"She does make good crepes," David said.

"And her little tattoo."

David shook his head in mock disgust. James pulled his goggles on, let them snap against his face, and smiled.

"And her ass. Damn, she has a tight little…"

"Jesus, do *you* want to date her?"

"Would it be too soon? I mean, I didn't really know how to go about asking."

"Fucker." David smiled. Both men exited the ski lift and James glanced up the mountain. "You going up higher?" David asked.

"Absolutely, my frail flower. I'm going on the runs they designed for the *actual* men." James didn't smile so much as bare teeth in a deliberate shit-eating grin. His eyes lit up behind his goggles.

"Yes, yes…you're a rock star," David said. "I'll watch over you when you break every bone in your freakin' body." And with that, James turned and disappeared.

The words replayed themselves in David's head now, gnawed at him. If only James *had* been here in the hospital bed next to him now, with every bone in his body broken. If only David had another chance to look out for him.

If only.

13

David's eyes opened. Another nurse was poking around. Constant fiddling. All he wanted was to be left alone. And to sleep. He liked sleep.

This one was blonde. Thinner, not so shapely. Her hair was pulled back into a bun, her face was narrow, and her nose was prominent, birdlike even. He wondered how many nurses there were in the hospital, how many were stuck here. How many doctors? She moved from his chart to the IV, and then picked up the phone, depressing a few of the buttons on the base.

"Can you let Dr. Devar know that she needs to check up on 509? Thanks."

She hung up again and started to walk away.

"Can I…" David started. His voice broke, slurred. His throat was still sore, his tongue heavy. He started again, "Can I…use the…phone?"

The nurse turned back to him. "How are you feeling?"

"I'd like…I'd like to make a call."

"The phones are out. Due to the blizzard," she said, shrugging slightly. There was the hint of an apology in her tone, as if she didn't want to be the one to add one more burden.

"But you…" He stopped short and indicated the phone, deciding that would be enough to communicate what he'd intended to ask. His eyelids felt weighty; it was laborious to blink.

"Internal calls. Our paging system isn't working either because of the storm. But the internal phone system works, so we use that instead. I'm very sorry. Is there anything I can…?"

"No," he said. Then he added in a slurred whisper, "Thanks."

She nodded. "Okay. Well, hit the call button if you need anything."

Then she disappeared, leaving David alone again, confined to his bed like a prisoner, facing another long moment of tedious consciousness which had recently only come to serve as a way station between much longer stretches of fitful sleep.

David let his eyes wander around the room. He wondered when the hospital was built. Certain elements of the architecture – the doors, the floor, the windows – seemed newer, more modern, while others – the moldings and cabinets – seemed aged, almost old-fashioned. It was an anachronism of styles that puzzled him, and added to the consistent throbbing in his head.

He pulled himself up slightly and, in doing so, realized how truly drugged he really was. The room tilted on axis and he watched as the double images crept in. It took all of his effort to lift his head and arm. Still, he reached for the phone, lifted the handset, and let it drop next to his ear.

"Operator," a kind female voice said.

"Hello?"

"Hello, Mr. Grace," the voice responded.

David blinked again. Heavy lids. Might be time for another nap. "I want…can I make a call?"

There was a pause and then the voice replied patiently, "I'm sorry, Mr. Grace, the phones are out due to the storm. I'll make a note to alert you when they're back in order. Is it an emergency?"

His drowsy mind filled in the scene and David pictured her sitting in front of a bank of cords and connections, an old-time operator, wearing a colorful flowered dress, her hair up in a bun, makeup perfect. *Pennsylvania 6-5000!*

"No, I guess not," he said.

"Can I help you with anything else?" she asked.

"No."

He reached out and replaced the handset, but before it even landed on the cradle, David was asleep again.

14

Memories have a way of distorting over time, jumbling dates and locations, shifting faces. David *knew* that James hadn't been in the cab with him that day, that chilly day in Manhattan when he heard the news. But the memory of who *had* been there was lost to time. It was another executive, another colleague, nameless, faceless, cleanly shaven, wearing a far-too-expensive suit and overcoat, maybe a scarf, talking on his cellphone, holding a briefcase; their faces all amalgamated over time. And so David's subconscious had substituted James.

It was only a few years ago, this memory. David was probably thirty.

"Deb, I know they sent the papers. I saw the email. You need to look again because it probably just got misfiled. If not, you'll need to go into Patty's email and print it. She was cc'd automatically." David was having a hard time masking his frustration; he had never been very good at that. Deborah Reischling was filling in for Patricia Jones, his regular executive assistant, and David didn't have the time or the patience for a learning curve.

"No, take Lexington, it'll be faster," James said to the cabdriver, and then glanced at his watch. "We're gonna be late."

David remembered the man's watch instead of remembering the man whom James was standing in for. It was a Vulcain black dial watch, graced with rose gold-tone numerals and accented in gold, with a black leather band. It was an elegant watch, yet not overstated. Still, David knew that it must've cost almost half of Patty's yearly salary. He liked that watch.

"They'll wait for us. It's our show," David said confidently, and gave a little wink. He was still waiting for Deb to come back on the line.

The cabdriver weaved in and out of traffic, coming close to an accident on more than one occasion. He leaned on the horn.

"Easy, buddy," James said, "we're late, but we want to get there *alive*, all right?"

"Mr. Grace?" Deb's voice was back on the phone. She sounded defeated.

"Did you find it?" David snapped.

"Mr. Grace… Sir, I actually just was handed a note. Mr. Grace, I'm afraid I have some…very bad news."

What now? he wondered. The lack of efficiency in the office when Patty went on vacation would have to be addressed upon her return. He sighed. "Well?"

"Right up there, the tall building," James said to the cabdriver, pointing.

"Mr. Grace, I hate to be the one to tell you this, especially over the phone like this, but…your father has passed away."

David took a moment. He let the silence hang there. He wasn't sure what he felt, exactly. He wondered how he must look to James. Had his facial expression changed involuntarily?

"Mr. Grace? Are you there? I'm…I'm so sorry."

"What else do you know about it?" David asked brusquely.

"Um…" Deb's voice was uncertain now; she obviously hadn't expected his reply to be so matter-of-fact. "Your cousin said that he tried to reach you." He had. David rarely answered calls from his extended family. "He said to let you know that he's taking care of all of the…immediate needs, but that you should come to Austin as soon as you're able."

Another prolonged silence. Then: "Is that it?"

"Um, yes. Should I – ?"

David hung up.

"You okay, buddy?" James asked. Obviously David didn't quite have the poker face he hoped he did.

The cab pulled up in front of the tall building. A doorman was ready to attend to them. James began to climb out, but then turned back and waited for David to respond.

"My father died."

"Oh holy shit, man, I'm sorry."

Another prolonged pause. Then James began to gather his briefcase, and push the cab door open. "You should just go. I've got this. You don't need to be here. Just take this cab right on to the airport, and go be with your family. Do what you need to do."

James exited the cab and turned back, still waiting.

David sat there silently.

"The meter's running, bub," the cabbie said impassively from the front seat, barely turning his head.

The meter's running.

James leaned into the open door.

And in this dream – this fanciful disjointed recollection, wherein James played the part of a forgotten man with a nice watch, and the cab driver spoke perfect English and called them "bub" like they were characters in a 1940s gangster film – David told James to go and do the presentation without him. He told him that he needed to go and be with his family, to pay his respects to the one and only father he'd ever have. In this dream, David closed the door and asked the cabdriver to take him to the airport post-haste.

But that's the funny thing about dreams.

That hadn't really happened.

No, in reality David had said, "Don't be ridiculous. This is a *huge* goddamn opportunity and we've been preparing for it for weeks. I can go after." Then he'd extricated himself from the back of the cab, paid the driver, and the two men had gone upstairs.

Only, David hadn't gone to the airport after the presentation either. The meeting had gone very well, and there was interest in moving forward immediately. The men they had presented to wanted their boss, Mr. Peterson, to lay eyes on it right away. Could David stay in New York a few days longer? Why, yes. Yes, of course he could.

David hadn't ever gone to Austin.

In fact, he hadn't seen most of his extended family ever again. The aunts, uncles, cousins, second-cousins; he abandoned them completely, relegating them to memories trapped in dusty photo albums, hidden away inside boxes sealed with packing tape, forgotten in the back of the garage.

David had never gone to Texas, where his father had spent those final painful years and where he had been buried. No, David had never said goodbye to his father at all.

15

The room seemed darker when he awoke. Had he slept a long time?

He felt his right foot itching and moved to rub it absently before he realized that it didn't exist anymore. His stomach dropped at the awareness. His foot was...*elsewhere*, all on its own, facing the slow decomposition that all his tissues would eventually encounter, just a little bit ahead of the curve.

Phantom limb, he thought, *so that's a thing.*

His entire right side was tingling.

He didn't want to get out of bed. He wanted –

the darkness?

– to fast-forward to the point in his life where all of this was normal, where this story was just an anecdote to be told at cocktail parties, a tale of surviving bad circumstances. But he had trouble picturing how that might look.

Just then, he noticed that the room was slightly different. What was it? The dividing curtain between him and the other bed had been pulled. And there was something else: the wheelchair had returned; it sat near the curtain at a slight angle, facing him. Just the fact that it was there, in the room with him, made him instantly nervous. Where had it come from? Did he have a roommate now? Did this *thing* belong to him...or her?

He pushed the call button. And the morphine button too, while he was at it, although he doubted that it really did much of anything at all; he had come to suspect that it was there more for a placebo effect than any actual pain relief.

"Is anyone there?" he asked in the direction of the curtain. "Hello?"

David thought he heard someone moan faintly.

He peered toward the thin curtain intently, hoping the emergency lights would illuminate it from behind, give him a hint of any movement.

Nothing.

He glanced out into the hallway, expecting a nurse to arrive any moment. Several people passed by slowly in the darkened corridor.

And then he thought he heard it again: a low moan from the bed next to his.

"Hello?" he repeated. He peered at the curtain again, moving the position of his head to find the best angle.

Still nothing. Not at first.

And then there *was* movement.

David stared hard, squinting in the dim light of the room. He thought he could distinguish the outline of a trembling hand, reaching toward the curtain, toward him.

"Hello?" he said once more.

He was answered by moaning. It was distinct this time, agonized. Was someone in need of help? He remembered how his mother, after her accident, would reach out to him, moaning his name, *needing* him.

The shadow of the hand grew darker, getting closer. It touched the curtain and he could see the fingertips tracing the plastic on the other side. He was suddenly aware that his pulse was racing, his heart monitor beeping rapidly.

Another moan, this one longer, more grating. Almost...tortured.

And then he thought he heard – of course, it was impossible, it had to be impossible – but he thought...he thought he heard his name whispered.

Daaaaaaviiiiiid.

David hit the call button again. "Who's there? Do you need help? I'm calling the nurse."

The dark shadow of the hand moved along the curtain, fingers rubbing against the plastic, slowly making their way to the edge. The moaning increased. And then the pale, quivering fingers came into his view, wrapping themselves carefully around the edge of the plastic curtain, gripping it tightly. David could feel his heartbeat in his ears.

Then, steadily, the hand began to pull the curtain back, plastic rings scraping along the metal support rod above.

David suddenly felt trapped. He realized that he hadn't even been out of bed. Injured as he was, there was no way to flee. He pressed the call button again, and then yet again, relentlessly.

Slowly at first, and then with a sudden jerking motion, the curtain was pulled away, revealing the backlit figure of a man. It lurched toward him in the dim light.

"BOOOOO!!!"

David jolted back in the bed, squirming away from the sudden invasion, but the movement sent shocks of agony surging through his brain. His teeth clenched. His finger hit the call button once more.

And then he heard something else: laughter. This other person was laughing at him.

It was a man about his height – which was to say average – with blondish-brown hair. The man leaned forward, hands on his knees, and let the laughter rock him for a moment. There was something familiar about the way he moved. He slumped back, letting his body weight fall into the wheelchair, and then exhaled. There was a broad smile on his once-handsome face.

"Who even says 'Boo?' Is that all it takes, anymore? Boo? Man, you're easy," James said, tiny fits of laughter still trickling out, punctuating his words.

David really wasn't understanding. James was dead. He'd been told he was dead. He had *seen* him in the snow. And yet, here he was, sitting across from him, chuckling. "James?"

"Hey, Davey," James replied casually. His face looked the same as that final image which had been seared into David's memory; a large gash ran down the middle, bisecting his features almost diametrically. It was like some grotesque superfluous mouth carved into the center of an otherwise appealing face. When he spoke, the loose sides of his split nose would flap and his mouth would nearly split apart. His skin was ashen. His eyes were dull, non–reflective, but somehow still full of the same life David remembered.

James was wearing the same clothes as the day they'd driven home from the ski slopes: dirty-looking jeans and a hoody, black Doc Martens boots, and a pocket chain.

James grabbed the wheels of the wheelchair and rocked back, performing an impromptu wheelie. He'd done the same thing when they were kids, playing with David's mother's wheelchair while she was in bed. David always hated when he did that. And James knew it.

"You're dead," David whispered.

"Nuh uh…you're dead."

Typical. He never took anything seriously.

"James…you're *dead*."

"Totally rude," James quipped, still mostly concentrating on his wheelie.

"And yet still an adolescent," David added.

James grinned and almost lost his balance, tilting backwards in the wheelchair a bit too far. Overcorrecting sent the wheels crashing forward with a bang. David wondered where the nurses were; he'd called them so many times.

"If I'm an adolescent," James said, sitting still in the chair for a moment, "it's only because you were always adult enough for the both of us, pal. And if I'm dead, it's only because you killed me."

"I did not. I just reached…I didn't. It's…it was an *accident*."

James moved the wheelchair closer to David's hospital bed. "The wheelchair's getting closer, David," he goaded in a sing-songy manner. David was reminded of Romero's Night of the Living Dead: *They're coming to get you, Barbara.* "It's getting *closer*," James continued. *"What are you going to do-ooo?"*

"Fuck off. Move it away."

James laughed. "You're the most responsible, most tenacious guy I know, and you have a fear of *medical supplies?* Freakin' typical." He wheeled backwards. "And yes, you killed me. I dissed your precious White Stripes, and you decided you'd show me what for."

"This isn't real," David said.

"None of it's real, buddy."

"You're not here."

"You were *always* very dismissive." James shook his head in mock sadness.

David looked at him, past the chalky pallor, past the grisly wound that bifurcated his face. It was James, his best friend since boyhood. The mannerisms, the inflections, the sense of humor. All there.

David leaned forward and spoke. "Will you, for once in your life…"

48

"Too late!"

"…be serious? Will you be serious? For once? Tell me what's going on! Why…*how* are you here? Am I…am I going insane?"

"Very likely," James said with a smile, and then he suddenly became distracted, fiddling with the metal pieces on the wheelchair. It wasn't unusual; David had watched him do this their whole lives. James had been a horrible student and had often resorted to this same cool, above-caring demeanor in the classroom, which mostly resulted in failing grades and too much time spent in the dean's office. At a time when ADD might've been a valuable diagnosis, he'd slipped under the radar, and had spent his whole life trying to make up for childhood glibness.

His whole life.

"James!" David said.

James looked up. His expression reminded David of a child caught drawing on the walls. "What? I don't know, dude! What do you want from me? Isn't *dying* enough?" The wound in his face separated even more as he got worked up; it unsettled David to look at it. "I don't know why I'm here either, buddy. But something's not right, huh?"

An understatement.

David could hear footsteps coming down the hallway. The nurses finally?

James heard them too, getting closer. "I'll tell you what is cool about being dead though," he said, grinning. He stood up from the wheelchair and moved to the vacant bed. "Magic!"

He pulled the curtain closed seconds before Monique – or was it Monica? – came through the door. As she entered, the overheads came back to life. It took both her and David off-guard.

49

"Well, that's promising," she said. She noticed the wheelchair and frowned. "Oh, what's this doing here? I know you have an aversion. These chairs aren't supposed to be anywhere near your room. It's on your chart. I'm very sorry." She moved it to the doorway.

"It's okay," David sputtered, glancing awkwardly at the curtain.

"And why is this shut?" she said, reaching out to grab the curtain herself.

David gasped faintly.

She whipped the curtain back quickly. But there was nothing there.

David took a breath.

"Did you *want* that closed?" she said, turning to him, her eyebrow raised.

"No. No, it's okay."

She moved to the clipboard and took it down off the hook, and then the IV. Standard routine. "You called me? I'm sorry it took a few minutes."

"It was…I hit the button by accident."

"That's all right. We need to change your bandages anyway. Get you all ready for some PT tomorrow. Fun, fun, fun!" She gave him a slightly mischievous smile.

David glanced over at the empty bed. "What is your name again?" he asked, his tone easing.

"Monica."

"And how's the blizzard going, Monica?"

She moved to the right side of the bed, pulled back the covers, and began to unwrap the bandages from his leg. "Unfortunately, it's still going strong, hon. No end in sight."

"So, you're all stuck here too? I mean, we all are?"

"Yup. Until the blizzard passes and they can clear the roads."

"Can I make a call?"

"Phones are still out."

Right. He'd forgotten. He was so hazy.

"And no cell service right now, either," she continued, "not that we *ever* had much cell service up here to begin with. There's a radio in the admin office if you need me to try and get an emergency message to someone."

He thought about it. "No, no emergency. Just thought someone should know about my friend James."

She patted his arm. "They already know, hon."

The nurses had changed the bandages several times so far, and Dr. Devar had been in to examine his progress, check his wound. But he'd still never really looked at it. He didn't want to see it. A part of him nearly glanced over as Monica did it now, but he refrained. He was afraid that seeing it – all exposed and naked and raw – was going to make everything far too real for him. And he wasn't ready for that. Not just yet. He just turned and stared at the other side of the room, at the empty bed, at the swaying curtain.

"Monica?"

"Yes?"

"Do you think you can up my meds?"

PART III:
THERAPY

16

"Rise and shine, sleepy head." It was a man's voice, deep and resonant, full of bass.

David's eyes fluttered open and he reached up to wipe the sleep away. His first thought wasn't about the strange new voice in his room. His first thought, which was often his first thought upon waking, was: *How long have I been here?*

"Is this you? Room 509? David Daniel Grace?" the voice boomed. David turned his head to see whom it was booming out of.

The man was large, much larger even than David expected him to be, but not overweight per se. Every aspect of him was just large, overgrown. His skin was dark; David guessed he was Hawaiian or Samoan. His short dark hair was neatly cropped on top, spiky, and shaved on the sides and back. The thin, perfectly trimmed goatee seemed rather small on his oversized face, but suited him. He wore scrubs that were orange on the bottom; the top was Scooby-Doo.

"I am your physical therapist. My name is Viliamu Moana. But if that's too much to remember, most people just call me Virgil." He chuckled.

Virgil. He seemed like a Virgil, David thought.

"So," Virgil said, "are you Room 509?"

David frowned. Was he? "I have, uh…I have no idea."

"David Daniel Grace?"

"Yeah. Wait…Room 509? Aren't we on the first floor?"

Virgil laughed. "The one and only floor, unless you count the basement, which I do not. Don't ask me, good sir. The numbers run the way they run. And I just work here."

"Are the phones still out?"

Virgil moved to the clipboard hanging near David's bed and took it down, then scribbled a few notes. "Yes indeed, which means no distractions while we do our work today. You're stuck with *me*, you lucky guy." Virgil laughed again; it was a friendly, zesty laugh and David found it hard not to smile when he heard it.

"Oh…goody," David said. "So, are you all used to getting trapped here?"

"It happens," Virgil replied, placing the chart back on its hook. "Not often, but it happens sometimes. It's all timing, really. Just like how you were lucky to get found when you were. Timing."

David sighed. *Lucky.* That word was being overused.

He thought about it. He still hadn't been out of bed yet, had he? Not since he'd been here? His timelines were getting confused. At some point, someone had removed his catheter and his IV. When had that happened? Regardless, he was glad to have missed that process.

"Let's see how you're doin' over here," Virgil said, moving around the right side of the bed, and pulling the sheets back. David still hadn't looked at the leg. He figured he wouldn't be able to hold off much longer. Maybe today was the day. The thought of it seized him and he felt himself begin to sweat. He could feel Virgil unwrapping the bandages. *Maybe today. And maybe not.*

"Very nice. Very nice!" Virgil chuckled. "You know your leg was shattered, don't you? All swelled up. It was dying on its own, I guess. You're lucky Dr. Devar was stuck up here too."

That word again. He didn't feel – not in any way – *lucky.*

"I hear you don't like wheelchairs much."

"No. No wheelchairs," David said flatly.

"Alright, but…it's gonna make our lives more difficult right here at the start. Can I ask you why?"

David thought about it but remained silent.

"Oh, so it's gonna be that way, huh?" Virgil's voice rumbled. "Well, I like a challenge all right. A little playin' hard-to-get. I'm down with that." Then he stopped and looked at David. "You know what my grandfather used to tell me, don't you? What you resist, persists."

David returned Virgil's gaze for a moment and then closed his eyes. "Is that some sort of…*island wisdom* or something?"

"Yeah," Virgil replied earnestly. Then he chuckled again, amused with himself. "Hell no, man. That's Jung. And I'm from Detroit."

David felt a little sheepish making the assumption, even more sheepish for making the comment. In that moment, every politically correct statement he'd ever made felt false. He was glad Virgil was not easily offended.

"You ready to do this, boss?"

"If I say no?" David asked.

Virgil smiled broadly revealing two big rows of immaculately kept teeth. "We're doing it anyway."

"Then yes."

"Alright, Mr. 509, I need you to start by sitting up. It's going to hurt because your whole body has been tossed around like a rag doll. But we'll go slowly at first, okay? And I'll help you. Just sit upright, and then we'll move you to the edge of the bed. Okey dokey, Smokey?"

"David."

Virgil winked. "Right. David Daniel. I remember. So let's just do this, David Daniel, okay?"

17

The crutches were hard for David to manage, especially with his contused right arm bandaged and sore. His entire body felt like one giant bruise, throbbing and aching with every step.

He hadn't looked at his injury, even while sitting up on the edge of the bed, even while Virgil had bandaged it back up with clean gauze. There'd be plenty of time for all of that, he supposed. He was in no hurry.

"She did a nice job on that leg, David Daniel. Did you look at what a nice job she did?"

"No," David grunted. He'd barely gotten halfway across the room. It didn't seem like Virgil was even watching his progress.

"*Your* amputation is *below* the knee. We call that BK. And that's *good.* You're likely eligible for a prosthetic. If we ever get out of this place." Virgil chuckled.

David was glad *someone* was feeling so lighthearted.

A part of him wished in that moment – as he struggled to make it across the room – that he'd just died in the crash. It wasn't the first time he'd felt that way, not in the slightest, but this time the feeling was intense; it possessed him. He was battling just to move, wrestling with an injured arm, missing a limb, and every part of his body was hurting in ways that he'd never imagined. But most of all it was the sense of how he must look to others. A freak. *A monster.*

David stopped.

"Fuck this," he said.

"Aww, c'mon, boss," Virgil said. "I need you to at least get to the bathroom and back this time around. You need to get to peein' on your own."

"This is bullshit," David mumbled.

"You know what they say," Virgil chided, "'What you resist....'"

The two men looked at each other for a moment, then David said, "Bite me."

Virgil exploded into a deep raucous laugh that seemed to shake the room. David couldn't help it. He smiled in spite of himself.

18

David found himself looking around the room, focusing on anything but what Dr. Devar was doing with his leg. He had gotten used to this dance each time a nurse inspected and changed his bandages. But they didn't seem to loiter quite as long as Dr. Devar did. David's neck was getting stiff from cocking it at an odd angle.

"So, I hear you met Virgil," she said, making conversation.

"Yes."

"And what did you think?"

"He's a sadist."

She sniggered. "You're fortunate. He's very good at what he does. Plus, it gets easier, and very quickly." She pulled off her gloves and moved to the small foot-operated wastebasket by the door, where she disposed of them. "David, your wound is healing very nicely and I think that we were able to save enough of the leg to afford you some really good options. At some point, I'd like us to talk about that, about the long term: prosthetics – which we don't do here at this facility, but should still discuss – long term rehab, vehicles, and yes, *heaven forbid*, wheelchairs. I know all of this is a lot to get used to. I want you to feel comfortable with where you're at for when you leave here. So, when you're ready, let me know and we can discuss it; you can ask me whatever questions you'd like."

He was quiet. He stifled an impulse to be glib about the wheelchairs. Instead he simply said, "Thank you." He was getting good at "thank you," and found that it wrapped up conversations nicely.

"Virgil will be coming back in again soon," she smiled. "Go easy on him."

19

Virgil called on David three times the first day. David dreaded him coming because he knew it meant pain. But he did enjoy the large man's personality. By the end of Virgil's last visit of the day, David actually felt like he was beginning to get the hang of the crutches. His body was getting used to moving around again after time spent bedridden. He'd even gotten his bladder to work on the third try. Virgil seemed pleased with his progress.

David hadn't looked at his leg, taking special care to avoid his appearance in the bathroom mirror, and thanking God that there weren't any reflective surfaces in the toilet area.

The day's activity had worn him out though. He found sleep easily and slept soundly. Which is why he was somewhat surprised to wake up so suddenly in the middle of the night. It took him a moment to realize what had stirred him: the power had gone out again, and the emergency lights had snapped on; they were dim, but glowed at the sides of his room. He couldn't recall many other instances where he'd gone from sleeping soundly to being wide awake with such little transition.

He could hear the snowstorm outside. The wind was blowing hard, rocking the old building. David looked around the room. He glanced at the other bed, half expecting to see James there, but it was unfilled. The room was empty.

He glanced into the hallway and could tell that the emergency lighting was on everywhere; it seemed to tint the hospital a subtle blue. He stared out into the corridor, half expecting a nurse or doctor to emerge, but there were only shadows present there.

Then, David became acutely aware of his need to pee. *Once you get me started*, he thought. He wondered if he should call the nurse, but then he noticed his crutches leaning against the rolling table that stood next to his bed.

He didn't like crutches either. In fact, he didn't like hospitals at all. The smell in every hospital seemed to be the same to him: a mixture of antiseptic and decay. He'd never really liked being in these places, even under the best of circumstances.

How long have I been here, again?

Emboldened by his last attempt with Virgil, David decided he could do it on his own. He sat up, turning sideways on the bed. His foot itched, the one that wasn't there. He hated how he could feel it. Carefully, he reached out for the crutches. He didn't want them to go crashing down. If that happened, he'd definitely have to call a nurse, and who knew how long that would take. He really had to go.

He shifted his body to the edge of the bed and placed his left foot on the floor, then slowly shifted his weight up onto the crutches. Just as Virgil had instructed.

Little victories, David thought.

He made it to the bathroom and out in record time – record time for him, that is. For once, he was very glad for the open-at-the-back hospital gown, which helped make his bathroom experience relatively painless. His arm hurt most of all now, and he was careful to skew his weight as much to his left side as possible.

As David hobbled back toward the bed, he thought he caught something move in the hallway out of the corner of his eye. He turned his head, but couldn't see anything in the dim, submarine-like corridor.

"Hello?" he said, not really expecting a reply.

David stared into the hallway for a moment, and then got curious. He decided he might as well venture out a bit. His bathroom escapade had been a success, and he felt like he had a few more steps in him.

He turned out of the doorway of Room 509 and glanced down the hall. Just then, he thought he heard a little girl giggling. Maybe that's who he'd seen. Maybe it was a child, another patient, who had wandered out of her bed.

David shambled forward a few more steps. The hallway was a bit eerie under the temporary lights. It had been hard to tell from his room, but from out here in the corridor, the hospital seemed much *older* than he'd imagined, a bit rundown. The hallway reverberated each sound of his movement.

He stopped to examine the emergency evacuation sign by his door when he heard the giggle again. Definitely a child. David turned but couldn't see anyone. *Maybe she's playing hide and seek in the shadows.* He wondered if she was even supposed to be out of her room. He glanced back at the evacuation sign, trying to get a feel for the layout of the hospital, but something about it didn't add up to him. It confused him. He wondered if he was looking at it wrong, upside down maybe. He looked for a "you are here" sticker, but couldn't find one. It seemed labyrinthine.

I'm just tired, he thought, *I should go back to bed.*

But he didn't. He was awake now. And inquisitive.

He made his way along the corridor, glancing into open patient rooms. Every room was lit by the temporary lights, running on generated power. For just a passing moment, he wondered how they knew the generator would last until the roads were cleared, until the storm had passed, until steady power was restored; it was just the hint of a thought, and then it was gone.

It occurred to David that he hadn't seen anyone else since he'd been out of his room. Occasionally, he thought he saw people asleep in their hospital beds, but it was hard for him to really ascertain in the dim light. *No one else.* It was a ghost ship.

He was more than halfway down the hall when he came upon a waiting room on his left, or perhaps it was a recreation room; he couldn't tell. There was a television and a radio, neither of which had power; a few couches and chairs and end tables, which were stacked with newspapers and magazines; a small table, surrounded by four flimsy plastic chairs; a couple of vending machines, older in style; and a ping-pong table.

"Hey, mister," the little girl's voice came from behind him. It surprised him, made him jump. He tried to act as if it had not as he turned to her. He found it harder to maneuver around like that than he'd expected; he was fine if he was headed straight forward, or moving in an arc, but not turning in small circles. It was something to work on with Virgil, he supposed.

The little girl was young, probably no more than nine or ten. She was blonde with a gap-toothed smile, and she wore her hair in pigtails. He could tell, even in the blue-tinged half-light, that her cheeks were dotted with freckles. She wasn't dressed in a hospital gown, but rather a ruffled pink dress, and it occurred to David that family members must've been here too, snowed in along with the rest of them. He hadn't considered that before.

"What happened to your leg?" she asked, pointing.

David cleared his throat. "I was in a car accident. What are you doing up so late?"

"It's not late, silly," she giggled, a slight lisp in her speech. "My daddy's having surgery."

What?

He must've heard her wrong. She said it so casually. Maybe she was misinformed. He wondered where her parents were.

"Does it hurt?" she asked, still pointing at the place where his leg used to be.

"Yes, a little," he said. "Where are your parents?"

"Do you worry that people are going to look at you, and laugh at you? Call you namessss?" Her lisp dragged the S out, made it more like a hissing sound.

"No," he lied. He was bothered. He asked, "Where is your daddy having surgery?"

The little girl smiled and laughed, covering her gap-toothed grin with a hand. Her eyes were tiny gleeful slits. "You haven't got no leg!" she sniggered, as if it were the funniest thing she could possibly say. There was a bratty glee in her words.

David felt his pulse quicken, his cheeks flush. He took a breath and responded sternly: "That's not kind. It's rude, in fact. It's disrespectful. Where are your parents?"

The little girl giggled again and pointed to a doorway across the hall. David moved toward it. The door was ajar, but only slightly, and as David got closer he could hear sounds, hospital sounds: a heart monitor and muffled voices, voices under surgical masks.

He didn't understand it. It was clearly the middle of the night. *Wasn't it?* They were running on generator power. *Weren't they?* Why on earth would they perform a surgery now?

David turned back to the little girl, intending to ask her if it was *emergency* surgery they were performing on her father, but she was no longer there. He turned, his eyes darting quickly, glancing up and down the darkened corridor, but she was nowhere to be seen.

Then David heard something else. A man struggling. From inside the surgical room. And the faint sounds of a man's agony, stifled, muffled, as if someone had placed a towel over his face.

David moved closer to the doorway and peered in through the open door.

The room itself was dim, just like the rest of the hospital. Several people moved around the table urgently, each one wearing surgical apparel: blue surgical hats and masks, gloves, and an outer surgical garment on top of their regular scrubs. On the table was a man wearing street clothes and sneakers, writhing.

David was perplexed.

Two of the medical staff held him down as he continued to thrash and...*scream?* No, it wasn't so much a scream as the hint of one. His body struggled back and forth on the table, his legs kicking out forcefully. But his scream seemed to be coming from far away, muted and slurred.

David pushed a touch further into the open room. And as he did, he was able to see. The man on the table had no mouth, no lips at all, just a smooth piece of skin where a mouth should be. The man's eyes were terrified. His fingers gripped the sides of the table. He continued trying to scream.

"Hurry, we're going to lose him," one of the medical staff said.

David was aware that the speed of the heart monitor in the room was accelerating, beating in time to his own pulse.

"I've got it," another man said. Moving close to the table, he produced a small, sharp, glistening surgical knife. It reminded David of the X-ACTO knives he and James had used as boys when they'd assembled model planes. Always so sharp. *So dangerous.* The thought was not comforting.

"Hold him down."

THERAPY

The two men on either arm held the patient down on the table as the surgeon brought the blade down decisively, somewhat forcefully, and began to slice into the skin on the man's face, pulling the blade along in a straight line, drawing an incision where the man's mouth should be. David recoiled as the skin separated. He could see a line of blood form and then drop away into the darkness behind. And as the incision grew longer, the man's screams began to emerge, violent and agonized; they echoed in the tiny surgical suite, and out into the hallway.

David felt himself gasp involuntarily. And as he did, the men in the surgical masks stopped and turned in his direction, examining him coldly, even as their patient continued to thrash and scream using his newly formed mouth, cut raw at the edges and bleeding down his chin. David turned and withdrew from the room, moving as quickly down the corridor as his crutches would allow him to go. The rubber tips thudded against the hallway tile, followed by the sound of his one bare foot in a somewhat steady rhythm.

The man's screams disappeared suddenly as if cut off. David glanced over his shoulder toward the surgical room. One of the men in surgical garb was standing in the doorway, watching David retreat down the hall.

David disappeared inside Room 509, hobbled into the bathroom, and locked the door.

20

While he was in the bathroom, the normal overhead lights flickered back on and the emergency lighting faded away. David realized that his palms were so sweaty they were collecting tiny bits of rubber off of the grips of the crutches. His breathing was rapid.

What the hell was that? he thought.

He took deep breaths, allowing his pulse to slow.

He looked at himself in the mirror, careful to keep his eyes fixed on his face. He hadn't really studied his face since he'd arrived. He looked older. Bruised. Tired. His skin was pale, almost ashen, and rough. His arms looked thin and his face was corpulent. *From a steady diet of drugs, no doubt.* His hair was greasy and unwashed. He needed a shower. A real one, not a sponge bath. It bothered him to even think of navigating that process with only one leg.

After a few minutes, he opened the door cautiously and looked outside. Not only were the lights back on, but the light in the room seemed different to him. Maybe it hadn't been as late as he'd thought. In the hallway, he heard noises. People were milling around. Not many, but people nonetheless.

How could everything seem so different now? He'd only spent a couple of minutes in the bathroom. But it seemed like hours had gone by.

Monica came in to the room and did a double take, surprised to see him up and standing by the bathroom. "What are you doing out of bed all by yourself?" Her voice had natural sass. He was positive she didn't mean any offense.

"I...I had to pee."

She shook her head. "You could have called me, hon. One day of PT and you think you're Superman, already?"

"What the hell kind of hospital are you people running around here?" David asked bitingly.

"Excuse me?" She was taken aback.

He indicated the hallway. "I went out there a few minutes ago and they were doing an operation on a man, cutting his..." He stopped short. Saying it out loud was going to make him sound crazy. *They were cutting him a new mouth?* Instead, he decided on: "They were cutting on his face. And he wasn't prepped or dressed or anesthetized or anything."

She looked shocked. *"What? Where?* There was no surgery here overnight."

David pointed to the hallway. "Right out there. To the left." He hobbled forward, and realized again what an effort it was. How had he managed a trip all the way down the hall? He pushed past her, and stood at the doorway. "Down there!"

She moved next to him. "There is no O.R. down there, David."

"Well, it was..." he started, but as he looked, he realized that he couldn't even see the door to the room now, the one the man in the surgical mask had watched him from. It wasn't there. Not like he remembered. He moved forward on the crutches again and stumbled, almost fell. "I'll show you."

Monica grabbed his arm, steadied him. "I think you might've just had a bad dream, David. We need to get you back into bed, alright?"

He wanted to protest. But what if she was right? Everything looked so different in this light. The hospital seemed newer, less run down. There were people in the halls. Normal hospital sounds. Maybe he *had* dreamt it. It hadn't felt like a dream at the time, but now, as he tried to recall the details, he felt them slipping away. He looked at the wall next to his door, at the evacuation plan drawing. It was normal now, legible, understandable, and on the topmost corridor was a sticker that read "You are here" right next to Room 509.

"David, c'mon," Monica said. She was kind but insistent.

After a moment, he nodded and let her help him back to bed.

21

He was ten when his mother was hit by the car. He was ten years old and the world – her world, at least, up until then – had revolved around him.

His father had gotten the call in the kitchen. David remembered him answering the phone, hands shaking, speaking stoically to whomever was on the other end, and then hanging up the phone firmly and turning in David's direction. It was the only time David ever remembered seeing tears in his father's eyes. His father hadn't been crying, not as such; there were no rivulets, no agonized sobs, no wet cheeks. But the tears were there, unable to be hidden completely, glistening, coloring his blue eyes a deeper shade of blue, and the sight of those tears scared David to death. They meant that something in the world had changed and it would never be the same.

He and his father had spent what seemed like weeks in the hospital. Seeing doctors. Meeting people. Peeking in windows where his mother lay dependent on machines. It was a blur; all of the images of that time blended together in abstract brushstrokes.

A parade of family and friends had marched through, even neighbors whom David had previously only met once or twice, and a few others who were complete strangers to him. These people suddenly became his keepers, his guardians for the space of an hour or two.

When memories of that time in the hospital eventually faded, David would still remember two things quite clearly. He would remember the orange-specked, low-pile shag carpet that covered the waiting room where he spent so many long days, sitting and reading, playing with his tiny Matchbox cars. And he also would remember one man, Smitty Cohen, a friend of his father's from the Army. He would remember Smitty – tall in his Army dress and sporting a blonde crew cut – not because he was kind or interesting, but because every time he would visit, Smitty would bring David a pack of Topps baseball cards and a bottle of Bubble Up soda. And so David remembered Smitty long after the others had faded from his mind.

The rest of the memories from that time period spent in the hospital were vague and horrifying and tedious all at once, and he embraced the idea of them fading away, hastened their retreat into the dark landscape of his consciousness where he would never bother to look at them again.

When his father brought his mother home from the hospital, finally, Smitty had been there to help him carry her upstairs. It had been a big undertaking.

"You know you can't stay here, Curt, not for the long haul," Smitty had said.

"Just temporarily," his father had replied.

David knew what that meant. They'd be moving again. Just as they had when his father was active in the Army. Just as they had all of his young life. And here, he'd *just* found a place to call home. *Just* found a best friend.

His father and Smitty had set the woman who was his mother by the front window in her wheelchair, locked the wheels, and gone into the kitchen to talk.

That was another memory that had never faded: the image of her there in front of the window for the first time, a dark silhouette against the golden afternoon sun, an imposing amalgam of metal and flesh.

22

David was pleased to see Virgil the following morning.

Morning? Already?

Time was running together. It had been ever since he'd reached for that coffee cup in the warm Jeep on the icy road.

"How goes the war, boss?" Virgil said. He came in smiling. He always seemed to be smiling.

"It goes," David managed.

"You ready for a little massage today, David Daniel?" Virgil asked.

David was ready to go home. However they sped up that process was fine by him. He was ready to see familiar faces. Smell familiar smells.

Virgil asked one more time about putting David in a wheelchair. David protested firmly. And Virgil dropped the subject.

As they made their way down the hallway slowly – excruciatingly slowly – Virgil chatted to pass the time. David vacillated between appreciating the good-natured chatter and wishing Virgil would be more focused on David's progress.

"So you know what I did last night?" Virgil asked. It was a rhetorical question and he barely paused before continuing on. "I got a book of phobias from the medical library, one of the thick books. And I looked up fear of wheelchairs. And guess what? It wasn't in there. That's how *rare* this phobia is of yours, boss. It ain't even in the damn phobia book!"

David grunted and kept moving along the hallway. Normally this type of conversation would agitate him, but Virgil had a way of presenting himself that didn't seem as if he were on the attack, rather just presenting information. Two old friends.

David noted that they were heading in the same direction as the "surgical room" he'd seen the night before. He was curious to see the area again in good light.

"You know what *is* in there?" Virgil continued, chuckling to himself. He produced a small piece of paper from the shirt pocket on his scrub top. "Macrophobia. That's the fear of long waits. Long waits! Then there's automaton…auto-maton-o-phobia," he sounded it out carefully. "That's a mouthful, huh? That's a fear of ventriloquist dummies. I swear to you. You can't make this stuff up. Then there's xenoglossophobia." He had an easier time with that one. "That is the fear of someone with an accent. True story. Someone with an accent. Guess they won't be taking many overseas trips, huh? And you know what my personal favorite is? Koniophobia. Guess what that is."

This time, he waited for David to respond, but David just grunted again and shook his head.

"The fear of dust. Of dust, for crying out loud." He laughed hard at that one. An older woman passing by smiled at him. "I figure…if someone can be afraid of dust, then you, David Daniel, you can be afraid of wheelchairs, and that's A-OK."

David smiled.

And then he stopped.

The room on his left was just as he remembered. It was a waiting room, or recreation room, he wasn't sure which. The couches, the television, the radio, the magazines, all exactly as he remembered.

He turned. The surgical suite with its door slightly ajar? It was gone. Nothing on the other side except for more patient rooms.

David looked back into the recreation room. "What is this place?"

"Just a place for patients to relax."

Inside the room, an older man sat in a wheelchair of his own, a tube of oxygen hanging under his nose. The radio was playing this morning: "If I Didn't Care" by The Ink Spots. The windows to the outside were boarded up here as well, but through the tiny cracks between the boards, David could see shifting shadows, an almost constant barrage of snow.

The old man turned sluggishly and looked at David, then smiled at him, a toothless smile.

Virgil spoke: "You okay, boss?" The way he said 'boss' this time was particularly deep-toned.

"Yeah," David said, turning away from the recreation room. "Yeah, I guess."

23

Virgil had helped David onto the mat in the small PT room. David wasn't particularly happy about the mirrors that covered the longest wall on one side, but he was pleased that he wasn't facing them. Virgil went about stretching him out, more or less in silence. David hadn't realized just how much abuse his body had taken until Virgil started to rub and stretch and prod in certain areas.

"Virgil," David said after a while, breaking the silence.

"Uh huh," Virgil mumbled, pushing David's left leg up toward his chest, focused on the task at hand.

"Is it possible I'm going crazy?"

Virgil stopped stretching David a moment and looked at him. His smile was gone, and he seemed thoughtful, serious. "What makes you ask that?"

"I don't know," David said dismissively, as if it were a silly thing. He was sorry he had mentioned it.

"No, no. Tell me. Something's going on with you."

David shook his head. "I…I just…I've been seeing things."

"Things like what?" Virgil asked. He continued stretching David out, but it was obvious he was paying close attention to David's words.

Just say it. Tell him about your dead friend paying you a visit. Tell him about the man with no mouth.

"I saw…things…last night in the hallway, but today they weren't there. I saw a surgical suite where there isn't one. But that…recreation room, that was exactly the same. I've just…I've had a very perilous grasp on what's real and what's imagined and what's…memory."

Virgil chuckled and nodded. It wasn't impolite or dismissive. It actually made David feel safe.

"Look," Virgil said. "You just went through one of the most traumatic experiences of your life. You lost your friend. You lost your leg. And you've been pumped full of so many drugs you wouldn't even be able to keep count.

"Plus, you're in an unfamiliar place in the middle of a snowstorm, the lights are wonky inside *and* out, it's hard to know what time it is because the clocks keep stopping and starting. There's no rhyme or reason to anything. We're just trapped here. Being trapped, all by itself, can be a scary, disorienting thing. But you...you've got all this other shit piled up on top of it.

"Do I think it's normal for you to have some trouble telling down from up? Left from right? Real from imagined? Yes, I do. And I think you need to go easy on yourself."

David took a breath. "Thank you."

Virgil stopped stretching David again and placed David's leg back down on the mat. His voice was calm, almost soothing. "All that being said, I find that sometimes, when things seem darkest, those are the times we find our light. So, if you're having memories, seeing visions of things, maybe it's a good idea to ask why."

David nodded. "Virgil? What if the things I'm seeing... what if those things are frightening?"

Virgil returned the nod and thought about it for a moment. "Well, maybe...maybe those are the things you need to see most of all."

David thought about it.

"I feel lost. Almost...I feel incomplete."

"That's normal," Virgil said. "You haven't looked at it yet, have you?"

David shook his head and turned his face away. He felt ashamed, but strangely comforted that Virgil knew.

"That's pretty normal too, boss. It'll happen and you'll see. It's not as scary as you think it is."

PART IV: ISOLATED

24

A nurse came in early. It wasn't Monica. Nor was it the birdlike woman or any of the others with whom David had become familiar. This was a new person. A new face. He wondered how there was anyone left in the hospital whom he hadn't met. How big was it? It seemed small. Where did they sleep? In patient rooms? How did they deal with being trapped here with each other on this...*island?* Did the normal hospital hierarchy stay intact? Was there in-fighting? Fleeting thoughts of *Lord of the Flies* darted through his mind, and the notion of the hospital staff fighting for supremacy made him smirk.

This nurse was younger than most of the others. Her dark hair was stylish, kind of shaggy. Even through her burgundy scrubs, David could tell that she was thin but lean and muscular. Did they have a gym in the hospital for the employees? Was it just the PT room? So many questions. Maybe he'd ask Monica the next time he saw her. Or Virgil.

She pulled down the chart from the wall and moved toward the bed. "I'm Tammy. And I'm here to change your bandages. How are you today, Mr....Grace." Her voice was deeper than he expected, somewhat throaty.

"It's David. And I'm doing okay."

Tammy smiled and went right to work changing the bandages, inspecting the wound, making sure everything was healing properly. He watched her face as she worked. Her brow was furrowed, her jaw set. She was determined, focused. David found her attractive.

She glanced over at him and caught him staring. He felt instantly self-conscious. He wondered if his expression looked as hangdog as he felt. Were his cheeks red?

Tammy just smiled. "Has anyone showed you how to do this yet?" she asked. "It's not hard, and you're going to need to do it on your own soon."

"Not just yet," he said quickly.

"I can show you if you'd like?"

"Not now. Thanks, though."

Tammy nodded. She looked back at him slightly longer than she should.

"Still no phones?" he asked. He was fairly sure they would've told him if the phones had been restored, but he felt a need to fill the silence, even though he'd been rather enjoying her looking at him.

"Still no phones," she echoed. Just as he'd anticipated. "It's still coming down pretty hard out there. I think we're setting some records, snowfall-wise."

"I don't think I've seen you before."

She smiled again. "I've seen you. I've been in. You sleep a lot. I mostly work the other wing, but Monica isn't feeling so hot today, so I'm helping out."

And then she winked at him.

There was something about it. What was it? She suddenly seemed so familiar to him. She reminded him of…

"Virgil's going to be in shortly. He's got big plans for you today, including, apparently…dum dum dum…a shower!"

That was welcome news indeed. David was beginning to think that showers were a thing of the past.

"When he does that, you're going to need to try to keep the bandages dry as much as possible, okay? There's a little bench in there and the shower nozzle detaches. It won't be as hard as it sounds. Have him show you how to do it on your own. Or I'll have to help you, and you may not want that."

Wait, was she flirting with him? Was there something intentionally sexual about her comment? Or was it a slip of the tongue? David felt his pulse quicken.

She turned back to the bandaging and finished up, then clapped her hands together in the air, "Good as new. Right as rain. Fit as a fiddle. Pick a cliché, you're ready to go!"

She hung up his chart and left, stopping only to wink at him one more time. And he felt it again, a pang of remembrance, of familiarity. It was confused, tangled up with an attraction that felt vaguely familiar as well.

He watched her go, snuggling his head into the firm hospital pillow. When she was gone he glanced up at the window, at the faint patterns bleeding through the boards, the endless onslaught of the storm outside. He listened to the wind as it escalated in volume, raking across the boarded-up windows in a howl.

Who the hell does she remind me of? he thought.

25

"So, what do you do for a living?" the young woman asked. David was trying to remember her name. The music was a bit loud in the bar and they had to talk over it.

Another memory. David was twenty-eight, maybe twenty-nine.

Dina? Or Diana? What was her name? He didn't recall. Diane?

"It's boring," he said.

"That's not an answer."

Her shirt was cut just low enough to keep catching his eye. The silver cross at the end of her necklace dangled at cleavage level. She was a striking girl and from the looks of it, she had an amazing body. Her hair was dark and cut in layers. He saw the hint of a tattoo on her shoulder under her minimalistic dark top. She looked punk, if punk were a thing that was safe. She looked punk-lite.

"It won't interest you. I'm trying to keep things lively here, make you think I'm a fascinating guy, and talking about what I do for a living is not the way to go about that." He smiled.

When he came into the bar, he'd loosened his shirt collar, rolled up his sleeves, removed his tie. His pants were tailored and somewhat tight. His shoes were Ferragamos, his favorite pair. It was a look that said, *Sure, I may have just put in a long day doing very successful things, but aren't you lucky I came here instead of going to the gym? Oh, and I own a boat.*

David didn't *actually* own a boat, but he did own jet skis. Diane, if that was her name, would look fantastic on the back of a jet ski.

"You're no fun," she pouted, taking a sip from the longneck beer in front of her, maintaining eye contact while she did so. He thought maybe she was being deliberately seductive, but it might have just been wishful thinking on his part. Time would tell.

"I'm a consultant. My company pairs fledgling start-ups with venture capital and we get a commission."

She nodded. "You're right. That sounds boring."

He smiled and took a sip of his scotch. "It is. But it pays well."

It was a ploy. He didn't mind mentioning his work at all. It may have sounded dull, but it also sounded lucrative, and that was never a bad thing when talking to a new women.

Her girlfriend approached. She was a mousy, giggling, mid-twenties blonde. David knew the type. He saw that she was trying just a little too hard: too much makeup, too tight a dress, heels that were just slightly too tall, her smallish breasts pushed up and together, her hair impeccably, strategically messy, her lips painted the color of strawberries. It all felt desperate to him, as if she were feeling the pinch, looking for a man to snag before her assets depreciated. She wasn't David's type. He liked her friend much better, someone more at ease in her skin, not trying quite so hard, not afraid to be aggressive.

The giggling blonde whispered in Diane's ear, giving David a once-over.

"I'll be right there," Diane said.

"Well," Giggly said, shooting David a sideways I-don't-trust-you glance, "just hurry, Dana. We want to go!" And then she moved back to their pack of friends.

Dana! Not Diane. Damn, so close.

85

"Are you being summoned?"

"Yeah, unfortunately," she said, pouting again. He liked her pout. "They're my ride."

David took a long taste of his scotch and licked his lips, "Well, if you want to stick around for awhile, I could always give you a ride home." He raised his eyebrows slightly and smiled at her.

Dana seemed to like the idea.

Dana. Remember her name is Dana.

26

They lay there a while in silence, Dana's hand stroking David's stomach. He liked her hand there. She felt small next to him in the darkness, and he liked that too.

He glanced at his watch.

"Crap, I've got to get ready," David said and sat up abruptly. He moved from the bed immodestly, letting the sheets fall away, and stood naked in front of the bed removing his watch.

Dana leaned over to the nightstand and retrieved her cellphone, looking for the time. "It's 3 o'clock in the morning. What the hell are you getting ready for?" Her voice had taken on a huskier, breathier quality that David found appealing.

He chuckled. "Well, I've got a conference call with New York in less than...*two* hours, and I wanted to fit the gym in first."

"Ah, you're a workaholic."

David shook his head and moved to the dresser drawer where he kept his gym clothes. "Now see, that's not fair. That's just a word that people use when they don't understand others with a different set of priorities than they have. If I were a dad and spent all of my time attending a rugrat, would you call me a dadaholic? Kidaholic? Familyaholic?"

"Sooo...you're not going to be a dad? Just work?"

Ah. She was fishing.

David smirked, but didn't really answer. Or maybe that was answer enough.

"You're not going to sleep at all?"

"Plenty of time to sleep when we're dead," he teased.

"I guess," she said, and then segued into flirtation. "So, you still have energy for the gym, huh? I thought we just got our exercise in for the day."

He smiled and goaded, "Hey, I only stopped because I thought I was wearing *you* out."

"Yeah, well…" She shrugged, a grin sneaking onto her face. "Maybe you were. It's been awhile." She laughed. "I'm gonna be sore, fucker."

"Sorry," he said, not really apologizing for anything.

"Naw, good sore. You know, I've seen you at the gym before. You go to 24-Hour, right? I recognized you in the bar. That's why I sat close by."

"Oh really! So, you're a stalker? Should I be afraid?"

"Most definitely," she smiled. "I liked you in your little, tight black tank tops. I was kind of hoping I'd get to see the rest of you at some point." She glanced up and down his naked form with mock lasciviousness and attempted a growling sound. "Never saw you there at 3:00 AM though."

He pulled on his tank top and shorts and gave himself a once-over in the mirror. He liked the way his arms were looking these days. He felt fit, centered, in control. After a moment more, he sat on the edge of the bed and began putting on his socks and cross-trainers. He glanced back at Dana.

She was lying there in the darkness watching him, her skin still glistening in a thin layer of perspiration, her hair a mess. A sheet was pulled up over her breasts in a show of false modesty. Dana didn't look so punk anymore. Not even punk-lite. She looked soft. Girlish. Even with the shoulder tattoo – a rose. *Fitting.*

She leaned over the edge of the bed and searched for her purse. As she did, the sheet fell away and David caught a glimpse of her backside, narrow but firm, a tiny butterfly tattoo residing on her upper right cheek. He liked catching a peek. Sure, they'd just been naked in front of each other for the last few hours, but this was different. It was stirring in a much more innocent way.

"Do you mind if I smoke before I go?" she asked, pulling an Altoids tin from her purse.

"Yeah, that's fine." He rose and reached into the closet, grabbing his gym bag and towel.

"You want?" she asked, proffering the tin.

"Naw, not for me. Makes me tired."

She shrugged. "Your call."

"Hey, just lock up when you go, okay? If you want to take a shower, help yourself. Just use the guest bath, it's cleaner." He started out but stopped in the doorway, giving her a decidedly non-intimate wave. She winked at him in return; it was a gesture that appealed to something within him, and he smiled. "Leave your number if you want," he added. That wasn't a normal part of his spiel.

27

Dana had been coming around David's place fairly regularly for three weeks. That was a long spell for David, especially with how consistent the visits had been. At first, it had just been sex. Mostly. And then conversation had crept into the mix. Then dinners. Movies. Laughter. It was almost like they were dating, but that wasn't a concept David was too familiar with, so he couldn't be too sure.

For some reason, he allowed it to happen. Perhaps it was because Dana seemed undemanding. She was fun, quirky, and could be feisty at times. But she didn't find reasons to argue, or protest. She didn't ask him where he was going, or when he'd be back. It felt easy. And he began to like her being around. To look forward to it. She relaxed him.

So, when she called him after work that night at the dance studio and offered to bring over Chinese, he said yes and was happy about it. It would've been easy for him to overanalyze that happiness, but he chose not to. Another day, perhaps.

They sat on the floor by the fire, her eating Kung Pao chicken in her work clothes – purple dance pants over a black, tight-fitting leotard top – and him dressed in light, loose cargo pants and a t-shirt, eating sweet and sour pork. They shared the wine, a Zinfandel. In the background, artists such as Cat Stevens, Joshua Radin, and Ray LaMontagne took turns monopolizing the iPod attached to the stereo.

At 8:15, the phone rang.

David didn't answer. Very few people had his home number, mostly just family, and no one he was urgently waiting to talk to. It was one of the reasons his home phone still had an old-fashioned answering machine attached to it. That way, he could listen to whomever it was leave a long-winded message, let it echo through his apartment, think briefly about picking up, decide to call them back later, and then *not* do that. It was a good system for him. He liked it. It worked.

The machine beeped, and Dana ribbed him about stepping into the 20th century at some point. It was a toothless jibe; in almost all other aspects, David's relationship with technology was cutting edge. His apartment was wired for sound, accessible by remote, had lights that dimmed on his command, and video accessible in both the living room and bedrooms. The answering machine was really his only connection to the technology of old.

Someone began leaving a message. It was his cousin. "David, it's Joey. I just wanted to call and let you know that your dad has been moved to the hospital again. He may not be able to come back home. It was just getting too much. He's too weak, uh…he's falling down. Listen, man…um, I really think it would be great if you could make it out here at some point. Um…he doesn't look great. He asks about you. Um…I think he'd really love to see you, and I'm sure it wouldn't hurt for you to see him." There was a lengthy pause, and then he added. "Just my opinion, okay? We all miss you. Call me." There was another lengthy pause, as if there were still more to be added, and then Joey hung up.

Dana had listened to the message along with David, and watched his face. His expression almost hadn't changed. Almost, but not entirely. His jaw set a little, his eyes narrowed. Halfway through the call, David leaned over, retrieved the wine bottle from the hearth, and refilled their glasses. And as the call ended, he raised his glass for a toast.

Dana raised hers too.

As the glasses clinked together, the fire reflected in them. Fire and red wine. It should've been romantic.

"Your dad is sick?" she asked gingerly.

He nodded, not really looking in her direction. "For a long time."

"What is it? Do you…do you mind my asking?"

"No, it's fine. Emphysema. He was a pretty big smoker his whole life. Pretty amazing what that can do to a man, actually. He was in the Army when I was young, he always seemed huge to me. Now he's thin and frail. And sad." His voice trailed off.

She paused a moment, seeming unsure of herself.

"You like the music okay? I can change it," David said, and scooped a large bite of pork into his mouth.

She shook her head. "The music's great, David." She traced the rim of the wine glass with her finger. Finally, she said, "You don't *wanna* see him?" She smiled, but it seemed forced.

"Naw, not really," he said quickly. Then he added, "My Pops and I don't really get along so much."

"A lot of people don't get along with their parents, David. But this sounds kind of…serious."

"Oh, it *is* serious. He's gonna die soon. I'm surprised he's not dead already. But he's not a quitter. He's a Grace," he smiled, chuckled, but it came off as insincere.

"What happened?" she asked, without hesitation. "Between you?"

David didn't say anything. His face seemed cold.

After a moment, she added, "You don't have to…I'm sorry, you don't need to tell me any of this. It's…it's private. I shouldn't have asked."

92

He looked up at her and his eyes were stony. For a moment, he considered asking her to go. But then the moment passed, and he softened again, took a deep breath in.

"It's okay," he said finally. And then added, with a chuckle, "Are you sure you wanna hear this shit?"

She remained stoic. "Very much."

"My...my mother was in an accident when I was ten. A hit and run. They never found the guy. He just drove off and left her there in the street. And so she ended up in a wheelchair, unable to move on her own, eat on her own, unable to talk really. She was just a...shell."

His eyes drifted off in the direction of the fire.

"Well, my dad was really big on this whole shared responsibility thing, which I get, I do. Everyone does their part. It wasn't like we were a big family to start with. But it was a lot...for a ten-year-old. Taking care of my mom like that. We lived on the second floor of this duplex. And he kept saying we were gonna move, because...it was so *hard* to do anything with her, anything that required getting her up and down those stairs. He kept saying it, kept saying it, but we never moved.

"Well one day when I was thirteen, I was taking care of her, and he was at work, and we had this window, this bay window. And he thought...he thought she liked it there, being set there by it, watching the scenery. So, I was this thirteen-year-old who hated having to be his mother's caretaker, and I must've forgotten to lock the wheels down that day. I did everything I was supposed to. I just...*forgot*...to lock the wheels down.

"And so I went in my room. And I played video games. Because that's what thirteen-year-olds do.

"But somehow…that day…she rolled herself over to the stairs. I mean, it was hard for her to move herself…in that wheelchair. At all. Ever. To do *anything*. But *somehow*, that day…she did.

"The one day I forgot."

Dana put her hand over her mouth almost as a reflex. David could see the tears in her eyes. He didn't know if that made it better or worse, seeing those tears.

"Oh my God, David."

"I heard the noise, a crash," he continued. He knew he probably didn't have to, but he felt the need to finish. "I had no idea what it was at first. I thought maybe a car accident outside. So I ran out. And she wasn't there. She wasn't by the window. And I knew. I knew right away. I saw her at the bottom of the stairs, the chair upended on top of her, the wheels spinning. I knew I should go to her, to help, but I couldn't. I froze. I just *froze*. The paramedics said it wouldn't have made any difference. She broke her neck, died instantly."

The tears ran down Dana's cheeks now. He wasn't sure what those tears made him feel. Envy, maybe.

"Well, my dad blamed me for her death," David said, laughing faintly, his voice taking on a more flippant tone. "He never came out and said it. Well, maybe once, when we were arguing, he might've alluded to it, but never really…outright. But he changed. Toward me. Everything changed. And I just… don't think I've ever been able to forgive him…not forgiving me. I was just a stupid fucking thirteen-year-old kid."

Dana put her wine down and placed her hands on David's, then crawled into his arms, crying into his neck. "Oh, baby."

"Aren't you glad you asked?" he said, smiling.

It made her laugh, and the laughter mingled with her tears. She pulled back and cupped his face in her hands, kissing him – almost violently – on the mouth. Again and again.

"Thank you for sharing," she said. "Thank you."

He slept well next to her that night. A soundless, dreamless sleep.

The following morning, he picked up the phone in his kitchen and started to dial his cousin's phone number. Then he stopped and placed the phone back in the cradle. A momentary impulse.

It had been the last time he thought of his father until he got the call in the cab a year later. The call that his father had died.

28

He had been drifting again.

His days and nights were spent drifting in and out of tiny patches of consciousness now. But the intravenous drugs were gone and he missed them; the Vicodin simply wasn't cutting it. His body ached, and the aches made it impossible for him to ever truly get comfortable, ever truly feel rested.

"Doesn't the TV work in here?"

The voice surprised him, but he knew who it was before he even looked. James was lying in the other bed, his body sprawled out in a casual manner. He was peeking out from under a pillow that was resting on his forehead, one foot on the bed and the other crossed at his knee. His hips were swaying back and forth absently, causing his crossed legs to move. *Like a child,* David thought. James was holding the television remote, pressing buttons randomly, thumping it against his palm. Finally the small television that hung above the doorway came to life.

"Success!" James said. "And look, Sigmund and the freakin' Sea Monster. God, I wish I was high right now." He turned to David, earnestly. "Wait, do you still have drugs?"

"Only Vicodin now," David said.

"Crap," James said, then reconsidered. "Well…"

James' face seemed worse to David, as if it were breaking down. James no longer seemed like a handsome man, marred by injury. He seemed – the thought made his stomach twinge – he seemed dead.

"What are you doing here, James?" David asked.

James looked hurt. "Niiiice! Real nice!"

"Sorry, I'm not used to hanging out with dead people. I don't know the etiquette."

"Well," James said, "you shouldn't knock it, buddy. I'm way more fun to hang out with than most of your living friends and you know it. Those suits you hang around with? Snooze! I mean, seriously. I'm hurt. I'm *really* offended."

"I just want to know what you're doing here."

James looked dumbfounded. He pointed to the television. "Dude, I'm watching *Sigmund and the Sea Monster*."

"Sea *Monsters*," David corrected.

"What?"

"It's Sea Monsters. Plural."

"But wasn't there just one sea monster?"

"Sort of."

"Well then…?"

"I don't know, James."

James looked at David and then back at the television, "That's nuts, man. All this time, I've been calling it the wrong thing. What were they thinking, though? I mean, it technically should've been called *Scotty and Johnny and the Sea Monster…* singular, right? *Or,* it could've been called *Sigmund and the Kids.* Wait, why did I never realize this before? Mind blown. Seriously."

It bothered David to look at James. Any time he got animated, the loose skin around the wound in his face wobbled like gelatin. He felt a wave of nausea, but looked away and took a deep breath.

"Ohhhh, I'm sorry," James said, taking note. "Should I wear a burka next time I come to visit? I'm sorry my *being dead* bothers you and all."

"James, why *ARE* you coming to visit?" David said forcefully, and then immediately regretted raising his voice.

James shifted to the edge of the bed and leaned forward, his face becoming serious, his tone shifting. "You wanna know? Well, all right. I'm here, my friend, to deliver a very important message. Something you need to hear."

David returned his look. He saw that James was serious and felt his breath catch in his throat. He waited for James to continue.

"David, I am here to tell you," James said, raising his hands up in front of lips, joining his fingers together, "that you... should *totally* tap that new nurse. Tammy? Wow! I mean, ouch."

David felt his stomach drop and slammed his head back into the pillow, frustrated. "Are you fucking *serious* right now?"

"I am *dead* serious. Pun *totally* intended." James was amused with himself. He rocked back on his haunches.

David looked back at him blankly. "You're a dick sometimes."

"Dude, seriously though...did you see that chick? Haaawwwt."

"No, seriously though, a total dick."

James snorted and then got quiet, an amused grin creeping onto his face. "You know who she looks like, right?"

"No."

James scoffed. His voice was suddenly loud. "Ha! You *liar!* You're a total fucking liar."

"Keep it down," David said.

James ignored him. He got up from the bed and came closer to David, crouching down slightly, dancing in place, playing with the strings on his hoodie. "She *totally* looks like Dana. So hot. I'm telling you, you need to tap that. For us dead guys. Can dead guys have sex? I really need to study up on this shit."

"Will you keep it down?" David repeated.

James stopped and looked around. "I'm the dead guy, remember? They're going to hear you *way* before they hear *me*. So, I advise *you* to keep it down, my friend."

"One, she's a nurse. Two, why are you here? And three, have you *seen* me lately? I'm not exactly in prime form." On cue, David whipped back the sheets, exposing a leg he still hadn't looked at himself.

James glanced at David's injury, then rolled his eyes and turned on his heel. "You're pulling the *amputation* card on a *dead guy?*" he howled. "Look, buddy, I know she's a nurse. But she's a nurse that was totally flirting with you, stumpy or not, and as far as you...well, I've seen you pull a whole lot better when you were in a whole lot worse shape."

David sighed. "And as for you being here?"

"Hey, I'm just saying 'hi,' pal. Don't be such a prick about it. You do very little to make a guy feel welcome, you know that?"

"I just...when your dead friend appears to you, it's supposed to be for some purpose, right? I mean, I've seen movies. I mean...right?" David suddenly felt the need to defend his position. "Aren't you supposed to bring me tidings from the great beyond or something?"

"How many times did I ever need a *reason* to hang out with you?" James responded. "But if you truly want some Obi-Wan shit, how about this? Fuck the nurse. I'm here to tell you to fuck the nurse. *Or better yet, talk to her!* And don't just let this one go because she's imperfect. We're all damaged goods, David. *So fuck the damn nurse!* It'll make you feel fit as a fiddle. Or...you know, pick your cliché."

David felt exasperated. "So, there's no reason? No purpose?"

"How the hell should I know?" James smiled, baring teeth. "Now, I've got to use the john before I go. But you think about the nurse. Hell, *I'm* gonna be thinking about the nurse."

He turned and started for the bathroom.

"James?"

James stopped, looked back over his shoulder, and grinned. It was an expression David had seen him make countless times. But this time it felt final.

"Yesss?" James asked.

David didn't really know what to say, why he'd stopped him. He felt like there was so much more that hadn't been said, real things, but he didn't know what they were. Finally he grinned and muttered, "You were wrong about The White Stripes."

James chuckled. "Maybe. Maybe not. But what the fuck does any of it matter now?" Then he turned and disappeared into the bathroom, closing the door behind him.

It was only when he'd gone that David quietly added: "I'm sorry."

29

Maneuvering into the shower was not necessarily harder than David had expected. It was exactly as bad. He found himself losing patience several times while attempting to navigate in such a confined space. Even the handicap railings weren't as much help as he'd hoped they'd be. He cursed himself silently, as he knew that his desire not to look at his injury was merely adding one additional hurdle.

"You almost have it, David Daniel," Virgil encouraged, his deep voice reverberating in the tiled bathroom. "You'll be doing this yourself in no time. Just don't forget to remove the shower nozzle before you sit down."

David maneuvered around slowly and then leaned the crutches against the wall just outside the shower curtain. He sat gingerly on the bench, making sure his bandages were on the outside of the curtain, and then pulled his gown off and handed it to Virgil. It wasn't easy wiggling out of the gown in that position, especially with his arm aching and its range of movement impaired; David made a mental note to switch the order around for next time: gown first, sit second.

He turned the dial on the shower and held the showerhead off to the side until he could adjust the temperature. Once the stream was hot enough, he began to move it over his body. He'd almost forgotten what warm water from a showerhead felt like. Bliss.

"You're practically an expert already," Virgil said. He'd put the toilet lid down and taken a seat. "You think you can do this on your own? Or are you enjoying the sponge baths too much?" He chuckled.

"God help me, I never thought I'd say this, but I never want another sponge bath in my life."

There was a moment of silence between the two men as David enjoyed his first shower since the accident. The room was filled with the sound of the water, pulsing jets bouncing off tender skin.

After a minute or so, Virgil said, "So, tell me about your buddy who died in the accident. How long had you known him?"

David stopped moving the water. He let the question sink in. The easy answer was: *my whole life*. He'd met James shortly after his family had moved to Sherman Oaks. James' family had lived around the corner. James had been the first person to say 'hi' to David the summer they'd moved in to town. And then he'd just never left. Even after David's mother's accident, when David's house became a place of speculation and rumors, a place off-limits to most of his other friends, James had remained, undeterred.

"I met him when I was nine," David said finally.

"Oh my..." Virgil said. David thought it was perhaps the first time he'd heard the big man at a loss for words. But after a moment, Virgil continued, and David reset the counter. "It's good to have friends like that. Long time friends like that. They really *know* us. Sometimes, they know us better than we know ourselves."

"Yeah..."

"What was his name?" Virgil asked.

David pictured James' face, but now it was hard for him to remember a time when it didn't bear a wound, gaping and raw. Every memory was suddenly imbued with this fresh detail.

"James. James McInerney."

30

David lay there in the darkness, feeling clean for the first time in....

How long have I been here, again?

He lay there and he attempted to think of his friend James, to picture him the way he used to be. And as he closed his eyes, he remembered the two of them at age thirteen, standing together in front of an open grave. It was the day they'd buried his mother, the day his and James' friendship was solidified.

There were so many people there that day. It was as if the hospital parade had returned for an encore and brought reinforcements. So many people he'd never seen before, or didn't remember, sobbing. His father standing next to Smitty, both in Army dress. And a priest – *a pastor?* – in flowing garments, sprinkling water on his mother's coffin.

James had been there, standing nearby. Always nearby. Both of the boys had been dressed in ill-fitting suits, sporting clip-on ties. James' hair had been slicked back that day; David had never seen it like that before. They had looked like – and *were* – young men.

David also remembered that his father never held him or even touched him during the service that day. In fact, he'd never even looked at him. Not as the pastor spoke words from the Bible, not as his aunts wept and pulled David's small body to their bosoms, and not as the coffin was lowered ever-so-slowly into the earth. Not even afterward, when everyone made their way to the reception, which was held at their tiny duplex. A hundred people or more, filing in and out, laughing as much as weeping, carrying large plates of food and cases of beer, and cramming into a space far too small for such a gathering.

At one point an aunt had asked David to play the piano and he had sought his father's eyes, but his father hadn't returned the look. And so David had declined to play. He didn't have any desire to play "Moonlight Sonata" that day. Not then. Nor would he ever again.

He wondered, in retrospect, if James had seen his heart breaking that afternoon. If he had seen David's furtive glances toward his father, his effort to be in the same space, his sadness. Had David worn it on his sleeve? Displayed it like a merit badge?

David had been standing in the kitchen when James had nudged him, smiled an impish smile, and led him downstairs. Into the backyard they'd gone, into the old tool shed that stood there.

"I stole this from my dad," James said, "and I thought you'd want to see it too." He'd pulled a magazine from its hiding place nestled in the back waistband of his suit pants, where it had been obscured by his suit coat. It was a *Playboy* magazine, badly bent and folded. David knew immediately that James had done it for him. Being a thirteen-year-old boy, and not knowing what else to do, not knowing how to say *I'm sorry for your loss*, James had done the only thing he could dream up.

David remembered loving the gesture. And loving James that day. As David's family was crumbling around him, James had been there to be his brother.

And so, they'd flipped through the magazine, sipping on Coca-Cola in glass bottles, and made promises about the girls they found within the pages, and high school, and what the adult versions of themselves would be like, and how they'd be friends through it all. And David, for the one and only time that day, on one of the most horrible days of his life, felt human. Felt real.

Felt like he existed as more than just a prop in someone else's grief. And it was good. For just over an hour.

That's when his father had found them in a rage, his blue eyes wide with anger. He'd ripped the magazine from their hands, sent James home, and pulled David along by his jacket sleeve, banishing him to his room for the rest of the night. And as David watched James walk away that day, turning and smiling a sly smile, all he could think was:

Holy crap, you got him to look at me.

31

David's eyes fluttered open. Had he slept again? Maybe just dozed. He was still holding the towel and it was making the sheets damp. He'd seen the nurses drop laundry in the closet, and he figured that was a trip he could make on his own. So, he decided to put it away.

The crutches were becoming easier, especially when there was no maneuvering involved. He was moving fairly quickly now, but cautioned himself against getting cocky.

He shuffled across the room and opened the door to the closet. A hamper was inside. He tossed the towel into the basket and started to close the door when he noticed his clothes – the clothes he'd been wearing the day of the accident – bundled up on the top shelf, wrapped in a plastic bag. And there was another smaller plastic bag there too. It held his valuables: wallet, watch, keys, cellphone. He reached for the smaller bag and stood in front of the closet, examining it. The watch, his favorite, was cracked across its face. He wondered if it could be repaired. It was a gift, after all, although he didn't actually remember who had given it to him. A work associate, if he remembered correctly.

He pulled the cellphone into his palm, doubting it had survived, but was surprised that it looked more or less intact. He pushed the power button, not expecting anything, but it came to life almost immediately.

Must've had the battery off this whole time.

David looked at the face of the cellphone: NO SIGNAL. Monica had mentioned that cell service was out – *or was it one of the others who'd said that?* – so it came as no shock. He put the phone back in the small bag amongst the other items and began to place it back on the top shelf when he heard a beep: the alert for text messages. *Curious.*

106

He pulled the bag back down and retrieved the phone. He didn't recognize the number on the screen. He pressed the button to retrieve the text.

"Call me! URGENT!"

David wondered how long ago this message had been sent. Who had sent it. And why it had come through if there was no service.

He glanced back at the phone again. It still read: NO SERVICE.

He thought a moment. If a text message had been able to sneak its way through, then maybe he could sneak a call through as well. He hit the call button and waited.

Nothing.

He pulled the phone away from his ear and looked at the face: CALL FAILED.

One more try, he thought, and hit the call button again.

And then the line came alive. Full of static. All he could hear was white noise.

"Hello?" he said, wondering if he'd made a connection. "Hello?"

He listened intently, hoping to pick up any sound. And then there *was* a sound. It was faint at first, nearly buried in the static, and hard to hear. But there was something there.

What was it?

He adjusted the phone on his ear, trying to maximize the volume of the speaker. And then he heard it, soft, but cutting through the static, and unmistakable: his mother's voice, low and desperate.

"Daaaaaaaviiiiiiid."

PART V:
THE ROOMMATE

32

"I'm telling you, I heard something on my phone."

Monica shook her head. "Then you'd be the only one, hon. There are people here desperate to reach their families, trying to dial out on their phones every five minutes, and no one has gotten so much as a signal. Not since the storm started."

"Well, I heard something." David protested.

"And what did you hear?"

He set his jaw. He wasn't used to having to defend himself. The idea that he was losing his sanity flashed through his mind once again. He had felt better about it since his talk with Virgil, but now he couldn't help but wonder.

"A voice. Just a voice."

Monica must've seen something on his face. She came closer to the bed. "You okay?"

He nodded. "Yeah. I…I just want to get out of here."

"You and me both," she chuckled. "I sure don't want to be up in this old place for Christmas. I'm a newlywed and I don't want to miss out on the first Christmas with my baby."

She reached under her scrub top and produced a picture of her and her husband; David could only guess she had hidden it in her bra. The picture showed the couple together at a Halloween party, smiling and happy. Monica was dressed as an angel, albeit a naughty one in a low-cut top, which showcased her ample cleavage nicely. A halo hung above her head, slightly askew; David wondered if it was on purpose. Her husband, a tall handsome black man, was dressed as the devil, sharp in a black suit accented with a red tie. The horns on his head were cheap plastic, and David could see the beige string easily against his dark hair.

"An angel with dirty wings?" David chided.

Monica looked at the picture herself and beamed. "Boy, you ain't kidding. He's a good one, this man. I'm a lucky girl. Feels like I haven't seen him in forever."

David smiled at her enthusiasm. "You look good together. Attractive couple."

"Yeah," she said, still smiling at the picture. "Wouldn't you know we got into a fight right before I came to work. And then the storm hit. No phones. So I can't even say I'm sorry now. They say never go to sleep angry, right? Damn shame. Shame on me." There was a passing moment of wistfulness and then she snapped right back and smiled broadly at David. "Hope he still loves me when I get out of here."

"I'm sure you have nothing to worry about."

"Anyway, I came in here with a purpose before all this talk of phone calls and husbands," she said. "You want the good news or the bad news?"

"Uh oh."

"The good news is…you get some company! The bad news is…well, you get company. One of the heaters stopped working in the west wing, and we have to relocate some patients until it gets fixed. It's getting too cold over there. So, you and the very nice Mr. Mahnung get to be bunkmates for a little while."

David sighed.

"I know, I know. You got spoiled having your own private place awhile. But Mr. Mahnung won't bother you much, I promise. The poor little man had a stroke not long ago, and he hasn't gotten his ability to speak back yet. Hopefully he will, God willing! But, anyhow, he shouldn't disturb you much."

"I'm sure it'll be fine," David said. He didn't *want* a bunkmate. But he smiled just the same.

When Monica left, David lay there, restless, waiting for Mr. Mahnung to arrive. He thought of Monica's picture, the handsome couple dressed up, looking cheerful, and his memory drifted back to another Halloween.

33

The party was being thrown by one of David's college acquaintances, a plodding bore of a man named Bruce Weider. For lack of anything else to do that Halloween – and also for the fact that David was somewhat morbidly curious about what had become of good ol' Bruce – he and Dana had decided to attend.

The two of them had been together – *officially* together – for almost four months, definitely a record for David. Still, he vetoed the idea of matching costumes; that still seemed a bit too couple-y for him. Dana had lobbied to go as "Bacon and Eggs," but in lieu of that, she'd opted to go as a pirate, a "sexy" one of course. David dressed as a Top Gun pilot, wearing a bomber jacket and mirrored shades that recalled Tom Cruise's appearance in the cheesy 80s action classic.

Bruce Weider's home was located in Malibu Canyon. It was not a large place, but it was impressive nonetheless, sporting breathtaking views of both the canyon and the Pacific Ocean beyond. David was enthralled by both the location and the guest list, pointing out Hollywood bigwigs and low-level celebrities to Dana, who really didn't seem to care very much. She suggested several times that they make an escape and enjoy a more "intimate" Halloween together. David liked that idea, but insisted on staying just a bit longer; he wanted to connect with Bruce before they left.

In fact, David was talking to Bruce when the incident occurred.

Bruce was dressed as a prisoner in old-time black and white striped pajamas, and a number plate hanging around his neck like an oversized bauble. His droopy cheeks jiggled as he spoke. In his college days, Bruce had been quite the football stud, but in the years since then, he'd allowed the muscle to turn to flab.

He was busy telling David about his recent promotion to development at Fox Studios. He bragged nonchalantly to David about the new comic book movie he had in development, and how it was he who'd brought the property into the studio in the first place. Bruce droned on, but the details were lost on David. Too bad, he thought. He knew that James would be absolutely riveted by the anything comic book related; all he could remember was "Green" and maybe, was it "Dynamo"?

Dana had been taken hostage by some of the other wives and girlfriends. They were gathered at the far side of the room by the patio doors, an assortment of "sexy" barmaids, "sexy" police officers, "sexy" cats, and so on. She watched David, sneaking in exaggerated eye-rolls and "kill me" gestures when she could: a finger across her throat, a gun against her temple, a hari-kari knife into her gut.

David glanced her way when he could. He was amused by her overt and melodramatic showing of displeasure. When she began miming a hangman's noose around her neck, he laughed out loud compulsively. Thankfully, it had timed out perfectly with something *somewhat* amusing that Bruce had said. Unfortunately, David's laughter had given Bruce the confidence to forge ahead with his ponderous anecdote with renewed vigor.

Dana mouthed something to David. He wasn't quite sure if it was "help me" or "*kill* me," but either would've made sense. After another fifteen minutes or so, Dana extricated herself from the group of ladies and headed David's direction. *On a mission, no doubt*, he thought, *to escape this place.*

"So what are you two boys talking about?" she said, sliding into their conversation, masking her boredom with eager interest.

David opened his mouth to reply, but Bruce's wife Jenny beat him to the punch, swooping in and seizing Dana by the arm. "Dana, can you help me carry some of this food onto the patio?"

"Of course, I'd be happy to," Dana said, and then shot David a wide-eyed look of horror.

As Bruce continued discussing his meteoric rise to the upper-middle, David watched Dana. She moved lithely in her high-heeled boots, the movements of a dancer; the tight costume complimenting her athletic shape. He smiled. She was not only the most attractive woman at the party, but also the funniest, most personable. He felt proud to have her there with him. He suddenly wanted to snatch her away from Jenny Weider and the other "sexy" hens, to sweep her up, kiss her hard, and take her home with him. But he knew there was plenty of time for that later. Right then, Bruce had a story he needed to finish, hopefully sometime before they were all dead.

Dana picked up the bowl of punch from the counter and followed Jenny toward the patio doors when it happened. David watched as her body froze, as she hung there, almost mid-step, straddling the edge of the kitchen tile and the living room carpet. And then the bowl dropped and the red fruit punch came splashing down, spraying the beige carpet and the pearl white couches nearby. The bowl bounced, upended. Dana teetered, wobbled, and then seemed to come back to life. It was as if she had been momentarily on pause, just long enough to do damage.

David rushed to her. She seemed fine. Completely normal, except for being flushed and embarrassed. He could feel the redness in his own cheeks. Dana tried to help them clean up the mess, but the Weiders protested. "I have some cleaner that'll get this right out," Jenny said. David doubted that. Bruce's face was sour; he attempted pleasantries but looked as if he'd smelled food gone ripe.

After a few more awkward minutes, David and Dana said their goodbyes and went outside where David handed his ticket to the valet. He vacillated between being worried about Dana, feeling sorry for her, and feeling utterly mortified for himself, angry even.

"What the hell was *that?*" he said, as the valet moved off to find his Mercedes.

Dana was flustered. "I...I just got tripped up on the carpet."

"No. No, you didn't," David said. His voice sounded more accusatory than he meant it to. "I was watching you."

"What do you want me to say, David? I made a mistake. People make mistakes."

David gritted his teeth. "Fucking hell." Even as the venomous words continued to pour from his mouth, a part of him ached for her, wanted to go to her and hold her tight, make sure she knew it was all okay. "You embarrassed the fuck out of me!"

"Oh, well, I'm sorry. Excuse me for embarrassing you."

"What's *wrong* with you?"

Her jaw dropped.

David had never spoken to Dana like this before, and he knew he was being petty, unreasonable, but he almost couldn't help himself.

"I think you need to see a doctor," he said bitingly. It was a comment designed to sting. He regretted it immediately.

"Maybe I already have!" she snapped.

David turned to her. There was something in her voice, a shift. "What? When did you...? Why?"

She took a deep breath. "I don't want to do this here," she said, an ocean breeze gently moving the fringe on her pirate hat, the darkness of the Pacific behind her.

"What is it? Is there something wrong?"

Her face was dour. Her eyes reflected the Malibu lights strewn throughout the landscaping.

"David..."

"Dana, just tell me, goddamnit!"

"I have MS," she said quietly. "Okay?"

David felt his stomach drop.

"I was...going to tell you," she said.

"When? *When* were you were going to tell me?"

"I just found out. I was going to...soon."

"What's this mean for you, Dana?" he asked. He wished his voice didn't sound so angry.

She looked scared suddenly, and tears came into her eyes. "I...I don't really know."

"Is it...?"

"The bad kind."

The valet arrived back with David's car, interrupting their conversation, and David and Dana quietly climbed inside the Mercedes. David wanted to say more, to put a reassuring hand on her leg and tell her that everything would be okay, that he'd be there for her.

But he didn't.

He released the parking brake, shifted the car into gear, and drove home with her in silence.

34

Mr. Mahnung was brought in around noon, just after a particularly adventurous round of physical therapy; Virgil had taken David down several new hallways, made a lap around the perimeter of the wing, and even explored the employee break room, which proved to be a virtual obstacle course for David to maneuver. Shortly after their return, Mahnung arrived.

Several nurses and orderlies, most of whom David had never seen before – *more staff* – rolled Mr. Mahnung into the room in a wheelchair. David felt his breath catch at the sight of it. The orderlies carefully transferred Mahnung out of the chair and into his new bed. One of them pushed the wheelchair off to the side.

"Can you take that outside, please?" David asked.

The orderly glanced at the wheelchair, a bit confused at David's objection. "Don't worry, it won't be in your way. I'll just put it over here in case Mr. Mahnung needs it."

David began to protest, but then reconsidered. As much as he hated the sight of the thing – the mere presence of it in the room made him feel queasy inside – he didn't want to seem completely unreasonable. He figured he'd just talk to Monica about it later.

Mr. Mahnung was a short, squat man with a comb-over of thin black hair. His face was gruff-looking, his lips were puffy, and his eyes were thin slits buried inside thick, bulbous eyelids. David figured him for late fifties, although he couldn't be sure how much of the man's appearance had been altered by the stroke, or even the subsequent drugs.

"He likes to watch cartoons," one of the nurses said as she turned the television on via the remote. A few clicks through the channels and *Tom and Jerry* showed up; they were on a beach wearing full one-piece swimsuits. David missed the beach. He had spent much of his young adulthood there, surfing and flirting, playing beach games with his friends. It had been far too long since he'd been back, and now the thought of it pierced him. He found it painful to imagine himself on the beach in his current condition.

"Why does the television work?" David asked.

The nurse looked at him, not seeming to understand what he meant by the question.

"No phones, no cell service," David continued. "Why does the television work?"

She shrugged. "Satellite, I guess? It won't work on generator power though."

David found the answer unhelpful.

Another nurse pulled the dividing curtain into place, hiding Mr. Mahnung. Then the nurses and orderlies departed, leaving David alone with Tom and Jerry, a mute roommate, and a wheelchair to keep him company.

For nearly half an hour, David lay there in his bed watching the cartoon cat and mouse chase each other around various locations, always with the same anticipated result. Every few seconds, his eyes darted to the wheelchair almost unwittingly. He wished it were gone. It made him anxious.

He wondered about turning the television off, or the volume down at the very least. He wasn't sure he could sleep with it blaring cartoon sound effects and fanciful music, and sleep had become his safe haven. Perhaps if he turned it off, he could plead ignorance when the nurses came in. He was a cripple, after all. Why would he have gone to the trouble of getting up just to turn the sound down?

He was busy entertaining the idea when Mr. Mahnung began to moan.

It was a wet and throaty sound, labored. And once it started, the moaning continued somewhat consistently.

Monica had been correct. Mr. Mahnung was indeed unable to speak. However, she was wrong about him not being able to bother David much. This moaning, a disquieting reminder of his mother, wheelchair bound and helpless, was so much horribly worse.

35

David's life between the ages of ten and thirteen consisted of routine. Mornings meant getting ready for school while his father cared for his mother's needs, getting himself showered and dressed, making his own lunch, and getting himself to the bus. Middays were about school. Afternoons meant coming straight home and taking over for the day nurse, caring for his mother until his father arrived home from work. And evenings meant dinner, homework, practicing the piano, and then off to bed again.

The weekends were somewhat different because on the weekends there was no nurse. It was he and his father. And his mother too, of course.

The afternoons were his least favorite times. It meant him being there with her alone. It meant placing her by the window, watching over her, feeding her, wiping her chin, changing her urine bag. It meant trying to communicate with her, listening and trying not to scowl when she spoke his name in distorted consonants and long vowels.

When she died, he listened to his father tell others, "I'm glad she is at peace."

His father said it a lot.

And David was glad she was at peace too. But he was also glad that *he* was at peace, and that made him feel horribly guilty.

The afternoons were quiet after she was gone. And in that quiet, David was able to realize how badly he wanted her back.

36

He'd fallen asleep, even with the television going and Mr. Mahnung moaning unremittingly. But when he awoke, forcefully jerking out of sleep, the television was off and Mahnung was quiet. The lights in the room had changed again; the generator was back in use.

Outside, the wind raged, and the boards on the windows rattled. David watched the shadows play and wondered if the storm would ever end. It seemed everlasting to him now, a way of existence versus an anomaly.

The hospital itself was still, as still as David could recall.

He realized then that his bladder was full, and so he pulled himself onto his side, preparing to make the sojourn to the bathroom. But then he noticed the wheelchair. It was pulled close to his bed, blocking his way. It would be almost impossible to maneuver past it. He wondered who had put it there, who had been so inconsiderate.

David leaned out to retrieve his crutches, never taking his eyes off the sterile, polished metal of the chair. As he pulled the crutches across his body, he shifted his weight to the other side of the bed. He'd never gotten up from this direction. And although it was an odd feeling – his body had gotten used to doing things a certain way – David had grown confident enough on the crutches to manage it successfully.

As he turned toward the bathroom, he froze again. The wheelchair seemed as if it had moved, as if it were pulled away from his bed now, more in his path.

David felt heat come into his cheeks. Perhaps it had not really been as close to the bed as he'd thought in the first place. Perhaps it had been a trick of the light.

He moved toward the bathroom slowly, watching the wheelchair as if it were a predator ready to attack, moving around it, keeping as great a distance as was safely possible. And as he circled past, as the mechanism fell behind him, David continued watching it over his shoulder.

"Televisssion," the low growl came, taking him by surprise. It was Mr. Mahnung. He was speaking.

David turned in the older man's direction, peering around the privacy curtain. He couldn't tell if Mahnung was awake or not; his face looked the same as it had before. David wondered if the man was watching him through the slits in his swollen eyes.

"Buuuullwinkle," Mahnung slurred. There was no expression on his face, no movement in his body aside from the pursing of his bloated lips.

David moved forward, inching his crutches along. He'd hit the call button when he got back to bed; Mr. Mahnung's doctor would want to know about this new development.

"Peeeeter Pan," Mahnung mumbled. "Peeeeter Paaan."

David turned the handle on the bathroom door – always a challenge due to the fragility of his right arm – and then shuffled inside. He turned to take one more look at Mr. Mahnung – still expressionless behind his nonsensical mutterings – and one more look at the wheelchair, then he closed the door.

37

David sat there in the bathroom, allowing his body to relax on the toilet. The plastic seat was cold on the back of his thighs and buttocks, but it was a nice contrast to the warm, damp bed sheets he'd grown accustomed to. From this vantage point, his hospital gown hung over his knees and hid both his nakedness and the porcelain commode beneath him, fusing them together in vague sort of way. For a moment, the image evoked the form of a wheelchair, man and appliance coalesced, and David shuddered, attempting, rather unsuccessfully, to brush the thought from his mind.

That thought, in turn, made him think of Mr. Mahnung's wheelchair, posed and predatory at the side of David's bed, seemingly moving of its own volition. And that brought yet another image into his mind: the long flight of stairs outside the duplex where he'd lived as a child and an empty wheelchair placed at the bottom, waiting for him.

His mother's doctor visits and routine check-ups had been an arduous process. Moving her *anywhere* had been. First, he would help his father move his mother from the wheelchair to the bed, listening to her groan at the invasion of her space. Next, he'd wait with her while his father carried the wheelchair downstairs; David would help her stay upright on the edge of the bed, his arm around her, her head drooping in his direction, her eyes wide. When his father returned, David would then head downstairs and wait by the chair. It was the walk down those steps that bothered David the most. He would take them carefully, one at a time, his eyes focused on the wheelchair patiently waiting for him at the bottom, as if it were longing for any misstep, anxious to catch him and break his fall. Once at the bottom, he'd wait in silence for his father to carry his mother down.

Getting her in and out of his father's Datsun truck was not quite as demanding. His father would transfer his mother into the passenger seat and then strap her in, and David would ride in the bed of the truck under the slim shell, just him and his mother's wheelchair.

Bang, bang, bang!

A knock on the bathroom door pulled David from his reflections and made him jump.

"I'm in here!" David yelled a bit too loudly. "One minute!"

David wondered who was trying to get into his bathroom. Certainly not Mr. Mahnung; given his appearance, David doubted that man had been out of bed on his own since his stroke. *Possible though, I guess,* he thought.

He glanced down at his gown and watched how it fell away just past his knees. From this position, it almost appeared as if he still had both of his legs. It certainly felt that way to him; his brain processed his right foot resting against the cold linoleum floor, right along with his left. David wondered if those phantom feelings would ever go away.

The rap came again at the door, a bit softer this time. *Knock, knock...knock.*

"Jesus, I'm in here!" David barked, beginning to feel agitated.

He could see a shadow moving back and forth under the doorframe, drifting unevenly.

Knock, knock. Quieter still.

"James?" David heard the name spill out of his mouth like a question. Who else could it be if not James or Mr. Mahnung? Wouldn't a doctor or nurse have answered him, at least?

The shadow continued to move under the door, faint in the half-light, and David watched it intently as he finished the business at hand.

126

"I'm coming out," he said. He immediately wondered why he'd given the warning. Was it for whoever was outside his door? Or perhaps he was preparing himself. As he struggled to stand, he became distantly aware of his own heartbeat. He swallowed; his mouth was dry. He moved to the door, and reached out for the handle.

"Hello?" David said. There was no answer from outside.

As he began to turn the handle, to open the door, he faced a moment of white terror as he considered who or what could be on the other side waiting for him. He recalled the mouthless man, the mocking little girl in pigtails, and his mother's own voice at the other end of the cellphone, nearly buried under the static. For a split second he was seized by an irrational fright, and then that fright quickly turned to anger. This wasn't who he was, who he'd developed himself to be. He wasn't some child who was permitted to be scared by shadows, shaken by noises, spooked by indistinct and hazy images he didn't yet understand. He was a man, an adult man, and men relinquish the right to be frightened of childish things.

David flung open the door, his dander up, prepared to exchange words with whoever was being so rude.

But there was no one there.

David glanced around the small room with the dingy yellow walls. The emergency lighting shone at the sides of the room. The two beds were just as he'd left them with the wheelchair standing in between, slightly askew. Mr. Mahnung was reclined in seemingly the exact same position, as well. And the unrelenting storm continued to beat and whistle against the boarded windows.

Who had been knocking, he wondered. Had it been a nurse? Had he imagined it? Had he been imagining a lot here recently?

"Soooorry." Mr. Mahnung's utterance cut through the silence of the room, taking David by surprise. David was confused at first, thinking Mahnung meant that he was sorry for the disturbance, for knocking on the bathroom door, but then Mahnung added, "Leeeeft," and David realized it was all just more of the man's confused and senseless ramblings.

David took a breath. He just wanted to go home. To be free of this place, and have everything be back to normal. Or as normal as his life would ever be again.

He shambled a few steps toward his bed when Mahnung spoke again: "I…didn't…meeean to." David stopped. These words came clearer than the others. It was a sentence. He wondered if maybe the man's words hadn't been as random as he'd assumed. Maybe Mahnung *had been* saying he was sorry before. Maybe he *had* knocked on the bathroom door.

"Didn't mean to do what?" David asked, looking at Mr. Mahnung's face. It was still expressionless, his eyes mere slits, his voice issuing forth from the puffy mass of flesh that was his face.

"Juuuuust…keeept driviiing," Mahnung said.

David felt the blood drain from his face and land in his extremities. He felt a tingling in his fingers and toes, even the ones that no longer existed.

"What…what did you say?"

"I juuuuust kept driving."

David felt his temple throb. He moved closer to Mr. Mahnung, certain he must have misunderstood.

"Say it again," David said, his voice filling with ire. "Say it again!"

Mr. Mahnung's expression didn't alter. His body was unmoving. But his voice began to even out as he spoke. "I… didn't meeean…to hit her."

David moved closer still to Mr. Mahnung's bed. Desperation was creeping in. A fright.

Men relinquish the right to be frightened of childish things.

"I'm sorry," Mr. Mahnung said evenly, almost in a whisper, any slur or hesitation falling away, "I just kept driving."

David felt his body trembling. His hands firmly gripped the handles of the crutches. He couldn't get any closer to the bed. He sat down on the edge, next to Mahnung's legs, and let the crutches fall; they clattered as they hit the floor, metal on tile. David leaned in, looking closely into Mahnung's face, grabbing ahold of the collar of his hospital gown.

"Say it…again," David whispered. He was so close, he could smell Mahnung's pungent breath, could hear his breathing.

And then Mahnung spoke again, not stilted as before, but full and clear. His expression remained static, but his voice seemed almost normal, confident. "I didn't mean to hit her. I'm sorry I just kept driving," he said loudly, and then he repeated it: "I didn't mean to hit her. I'm sorry I just kept driving. I didn't mean to hit her. I'm sorry I just kept driving."

David felt the gooseflesh rise on his arms, felt his scalp bristle, his lips quiver. His grip tightened on the collar as the man repeated the same words over and over, his speed increasing, his voice rising in volume and intensity.

"Say it again," David whispered. "Say it, you motherfucker!"

"I didn't mean to hit her. I'm sorry I just kept driving. I didn't mean to hit her. I'm sorry I just kept driving." Mahnung sounded like a child's toy, set on repeat, his tone rising, his face expressionless; a broken, taunting jack-in-the-box gone haywire. "I didn't mean to hit her. I'm sorry I just kept driving. I didn't mean to hit her. I'm sorry I just kept driving."

David felt the heat rise in his cheeks. His hands were balled into ever tightening fists, gripping the fabric of the gown, shaking. The impulse to strike came suddenly, and he pulled his right arm back despite its injuries. Without even bothering to release the gown, David brought his fist into Mahnung's bloated mass of a face, striking him hard on the cheek. "Say it...again!"

With nary a pause to recover from the blow, Mahnung continued. "I didn't mean to hit her. I'm sorry I just kept driving."

"You hit my mother! You left her there!" David's left fist came down.

Mahnung's face whipped to the right, his lips pursing. "I didn't mean to hit her."

Another punch from David. And then another. His initial impulse to strike the man quickly devolved into a frenzy. He felt his knuckles connect against the man's fleshy face, striking the bones hidden somewhere underneath. He felt the wetness on his fingers, saw the smears of blood on Mahnung's face, and on the pillow. But he didn't stop.

The heart monitor alarm sounded.

"I'm ssssorry...I jusssth kepth driving," Mahnung gasped through deformed, bloodied lips and gums, a sickening, sputtering wetness wrapped around every word. "I didn'th... mean...thoo hith her."

130

David raised his right hand again and brought it down hard. And then the left, feeling his own pain, overcome, animalistic.

Several machines were beeping now.

Mahnung's face was a pulp. He opened his mouth to speak, and David's fist connected with it again. Even when no more words came to Mahnung's lips, David continued to strike mercilessly.

"You killed her, you *motherfucker!*"

It was only the arrival of the hospital staff that saved Mr. Mahnung's life. A large pair of hands pulled David up and away from the bed like a ragdoll, held him tightly. A doctor and two nurses pushed past. David heard someone murmur, "Oh my dear God." And then all movement went into a fuzzy slow motion.

As David was dropped onto his own bed, held in place there, he simply gazed at Mahnung's battered face with a mixture of sickness, regret, pity, contempt, and most of all, satisfaction.

It was then he noticed the old woman standing in the doorway. She was dressed in black, looking in the direction of Mr. Mahnung. David recognized her. He'd seen her on the first day in the hospital; she had smiled at him kindly then. But now, her face was troubled, despondent. David wondered if she'd seen him striking Mr. Mahnung, if she'd seen the gratification on his face as he did it.

The old woman turned toward David, looked at him a moment, then shook her head softly, turned, and disappeared into the dimness of the hallway. And as she went, David felt the satisfaction drain away, until all that was left was a cold, bleak feeling in the center of his gut.

PART VI:
HAUNTED

38

Mr. Mahnung had been moved out of Room 509 quickly, leaving David alone again. He propped himself up slightly and watched the activity in the hallway; doctors and nurses scurried about, flustered, while one of the larger orderlies stood outside of his room, guarding it.

"They're deciding what to do with you."

David recognized James' voice before even seeing him emerge from the bathroom. Well, not emerge as much as lean into the room and loiter there, half in and half out. James was looking even worse than the last time David saw him. David wondered if James' tissue was decomposing; his body seemed to be breaking down before his eyes.

"That man killed my mother," David responded. There was little passion in his voice now; he was quiet but forthright.

James scoffed. He reached up with one hand to rub it through his hair, and as he did, David swore that he could see tiny bits of James' skin flaking away. James' facial wound wasn't pliable anymore, nor did it jiggle; it seemed hard and unmoving, rigid, scabrous. "What makes you think that, Davey?"

Davey. Dear lord, David hated the nickname "Davey." No one else had ever been able to call him "Davey." And James only got away with it because David *knew* that any protestation on his part would likely only result in an obstinate increase in James' usage.

"He confessed. He said he left her there. He just left her there, James."

James looked over at David, head tilted down, his dull eyes peering out from under his brow line, his eyebrows raised in an incredulous manner. "And he's here in this hospital? The man who hit your mother? In the bed next to yours? Don't you think that would be…an *amazing* coincidence?"

Yes.

Yes, David did think that. But he also knew that stranger things had happened. The universe worked in mysterious ways. At least that's what he chose to believe in that moment. Perhaps that was the reason all of this had happened. Perhaps it was the reason he was there.

But he said none of those things out loud to James. He remained stoic.

"They're trying to decide if they should lock you up, buddy," James said, looking cursorily toward the hallway.

David watched Dr. Devar getting a rundown from some of the others, those who had been there and seen what had happened. It was all hushed whispers and furtive glances. But David felt confident that they'd see his side – that he'd be *vindicated* – once they listened to his story.

"You know what I think?" James continued. "I think you need to get your head out of your ass and start seeing things the way they are, and not how you *want* them to be."

The comment angered David. He didn't like being challenged, especially not by James. His jaw clenched and he focused his gaze on the activity in the hallway, attempting to ignore the comment, to ignore James completely. But as much as he tried, David couldn't deny his growing frustration.

Get your head out of your ass? He is one to talk!

Finally, he turned and barked, "So, you think I want…?!" But, James was already gone. Only the empty doorway remained, the door half open.

136

Just then, the overhead lights flickered back to life and the emergency lighting faded away again. At that same moment, Dr. Devar entered the room, followed close behind by Virgil and then Monica, trailing the pack.

The A-Listers, David thought.

Their expressions were dour. He knew how this must look to all of them but was confident that they'd understand once he had a chance to explain everything. Virgil took a seat on the opposite bed; it creaked under his large mass. Monica stood off to the side near the wall, her left hand tucked under her right armpit, her right hand near her mouth; she was biting her nails a bit, nervously. Dr. Devar stood near David's bed and looked at him.

"How are you, David?" she asked. Her expression was earnest, austere, perhaps even a little pleading.

David nodded. It was a quick, confident movement. He felt good, assured. He kept his chin up, his face presented to them. Justified.

"David, we're all very troubled about what happened here today," Devar continued. "These kinds of violent outbursts... We're working with a very minimal crew up here, a skeleton crew really, and we're working long hours until the storm clears. It is taxing to begin with. And the truth is...we don't have the staff or the facilities..."

David shook his head, his eyes finding hers. "*I'm* not dangerous. *That man* is dangerous. *That man* is a killer." There was a quaver in his voice that discomfited him.

Dr. Devar exchanged surprised looks with the others. Virgil looked shocked. Monica seemed like a deer in headlights. "I'm sorry. I don't understand. What do you mean by that?" Dr. Devar asked.

"That man killed – or, he permanently *disabled* – my mother when I was ten years old. He *left her to die* in the street. And that *led* to her death three years later. He confessed to it. He told me he was sorry. He kept repeating it."

There was a confused silence in the room, another round of puzzled glances back and forth.

"David," Dr. Devar said – she was speaking slowly now, carefully, patiently, as if to a child. "David, that's…simply not possible."

"He told me!" David interrupted. He was surprised by the volume of his words. He had wanted this to remain unemotional. It would be better if it were unemotional. Just the facts.

Dr. Devar looked over to Virgil again. Virgil leaned forward slightly and spoke. His voice seemed even deeper than usual, more resonant, if that were possible; perhaps it was his subdued tone. "Mr. Mahnung is a tourist. He is here from Germany for the first time in his life. He was on vacation with his wife when he suffered a stroke. There's…*no way* he could've run down your mother when you were ten, boss."

David felt a bitter confusion wash over him, a cognitive dissonance between the words he was hearing and what he *knew* in his gut to be true, what simply *must* be true.

"But…he told me…"

Virgil shook his head slowly, his face fixed.

Dr. Devar said, "Mr. Mahnung has no verbal function at this time, David. If you heard words, they were meaningless. I've examined him and there seems to be no connection between anything he's saying and anything he might be trying to convey."

David looked from Dr. Devar to Virgil, and then to Monica. He realized that Monica, in particular, seemed frightened of him now. She glanced at him awkwardly, surreptitiously. She regarded him as if he were a monster.

"I'm not...crazy," David said. But he had a hard time believing his own words.

Virgil replied, "We don't think you are, boss. We think you may be suffering from...some acute case of PTSD, maybe. You've gone through a lot recently with the accident, losing your friend, and your leg...that can take its toll on a man."

Monica nodded anxiously and continued to bite her nails.

Dr. Devar added, "David, Mr. Mahnung *will* be okay. But you hurt him pretty badly; you broke his nose, some teeth, some bones in his face. What you did to him was frightening, David – *savage* – even if you *did* think you were exacting some sort of revenge. However, Mr. Mahnung will heal. And we're more concerned, right now, about your state of mind. About what to do with *you*. We don't *want* to put you under lock and key, to keep you *guarded*, but please understand that we will if we must."

David took a deep breath. His hands were shaking again. How had it all gotten so twisted? And so quickly? Was it possible that he'd assaulted a completely innocent man, a tourist recovering from a stroke? Was it possible that *David* was the bad guy here?

"Oh God..." he said softly. "How...then why did he...? Oh God..."

Dr. Devar nodded to Virgil and then turned back to David. "Monica and I are going to step out and leave you and Virgil to talk for a few minutes. I want you to know that we're trying to do what's best for you, David. We're not the enemy. Everyone here only wants what's *best for you.* I hope you believe that."

As the two women left the room, Monica glanced back over her shoulder at David again. It was the same look as before: fear. She was afraid of him, repelled by him, even. When had that happened? When had he become the monster?

39

"When did you become such a goddamn terror?" his father asked.

David was sixteen, but was quickly approaching his seventeenth birthday, which meant it was nearly spring. And he'd been suspended from school. Again. For fighting. Again.

"You know, life hasn't exactly been a bowl of cherries since your mother got hit by that car, David. One would think an intelligent young man like you wouldn't go trying to make things even harder on us!" His father's blue eyes were wide, a combination of fury and enervating fatigue.

"You always told me to stand up for myself," David whispered. He didn't give the old man the satisfaction of an extreme reaction. There would be no anger. No temper tantrum. No raised voices. His tone was flat, emotionless, matter-of-fact.

His father shook his head and sat down across from David at the kitchen table. The letter that detailed David's suspension from school was still held tightly in his hand.

"When you have to stand up for yourself *this much*… well, at some point, you have to look at what *you're* contributing. I mean…for God's sake, David, are people really going out of their way to *pick on you?* You're on the goddamn football team. You're on the student government. Christ, you *were* on your way to being valedictorian!"

"I still am," David said dispassionately.

"Yeah well," his father started, looking at the slightly crumpled paper in his hand, "you won't be doing *any* of these things if this shit continues."

David sat there in silence, his eyes down at the table.

"I mean, listen to this, David," his father said, and then began to read from the letter. "'David exhibits more academic potential than any student in recent memory. Unfortunately, he also exhibits more anger. If his lack of restraint and impulse control continues unabated, his actions stand to seriously affect both his academic career and future collegiate and professional opportunities.'"

David couldn't help but smile at the term "academic career."

His father slammed the paper down on the kitchen table. He did it hard enough to make the salt and pepper dispensers rattle. "You think this is funny?" he snapped.

"No, sir," David said formally. He knew his father went in for any of that respectful Army crap. He made sure that there was no obvious trace of impertinence behind his words.

"Well, you better not. You think I'm always going to be here? Always going to be around to take care of you?"

No, David did *not* think that. He barely registered the old man's presence as it was.

"Well, if you're suspended from school, then...you're going to work around here. No day off. You can start by cleaning the truck, wash *and* wax, and then the bathrooms. Spotless. You've got two hours. Then you come see me and we'll figure out what's next on the list. You got that?"

"Yes, sir."

His father looked at him a long moment, his eyes unblinking. He shook his head, gripping the paper. "You break my fuckin' heart sometimes, you know that? You have...all this potential, all this intelligence. You're a good-looking, healthy kid. But what good is all of that if you're always so goddamned angry all the time? It's like this mist that hangs around your head, blinding you to everything. Well, you may not see it right now. And you may think I'm just a stupid old man who doesn't know shit, but I'll tell you this, and you can mark it down. Things won't change until you do."

DARK AND BROKEN THINGS

40

"So, what's it going to be, boss?" Virgil asked. "Are we going to have to worry about you?"

David shook his head. He didn't know what to feel, what to say. If he told Virgil that he felt unhinged they'd surely lock him away or post a guard. He didn't want to feel even more like a prisoner here than he already did.

"Dr. Devar isn't lying," Virgil went on. "There're a lot of people here very worried about you. Very…*concerned*…that you might not be making the best choices."

"This *place* is making me crazy," David said finally. It seemed like a good compromise. The words felt right coming out of his mouth. Why hadn't he thought of it before? It wasn't *him*, it was the circumstances, the isolation, this *place*.

"This place?" Virgil echoed him, frowning. "This *place* saved you, boss. And the people in this place are tryin' *very hard*. They're tryin' to make you *whole* again. And I'm very worried you don't see that."

"And I'm worried that you don't appreciate how nuts this all is for me!" David said, his voice shaking. "Don't *you see* how I went from being a normal guy on his way home from a ski trip with his friend to being here, half of a person, in this place with the windows and doors boarded up, the lights going haywire? And my friend is dead. And my life as I knew it is over. And then they bring that man in here, and he says…he says *those things*…. I'm right on the edge, Virgil. Am I losing it a little bit? Yeah, I guess I am. But, am I dangerous? No, I'm not. What happened…with that man…that was…a mistake. But… *nothing* like that is going to happen again."

Virgil listened to him, his expression earnest. He allowed David's words to hang in the air.

David returned Virgil's look and suddenly it seemed like his words hadn't been enough, like he hadn't said the right things. The perception frustrated him, brought a renewed heat into his cheeks. He added, finally, curtly, "I've been through a lot, is all I'm saying. And I think all of you people need to give me a fuckin' break."

Virgil continued looking at David, listening to him, his brow furrowed. After a moment, he nodded and spoke softly. "I hear you. I hear you, I do. But I sit here and I can't help but wonder…when your last *truly* happy memory was."

David's thoughts jumped immediately to recent events. To James. Skiing. The lodge. The annual trip. But that wasn't it. Not truly. It was Dana. That was the last time he was truly happy. He quickly moved away from the thought.

"Do you know who Meister Eckhart is?" Virgil asked.

David shook his head.

"Eckhart was a German philosopher. I may have a book of his around here. I think you might like it."

"Okay…" David sighed. He didn't see how this applied. It was obvious that Virgil was leading to a point and David wished he'd just arrive at it.

Virgil continued, "Eckhart said a lot of things. But one of the things I really love is this. He said, 'If the only prayer you ever say in your entire life is thank you, it will be enough.'"

David scrutinized Virgil's face. For the big man to be quoting some philosopher at a time like this felt trite to David, and he was beginning to get frustrated with the whole conversation. He writhed in his bed, uncomfortably.

Virgil leaned forward, cleared his throat, and continued to speak, his voice deep and soft, his words measured. There was a sincerity in his face, a kindness in his manner.

"When you open your eyes, David Daniel, when you draw breath in the morning, say thank you. When someone tries to help you up, to make you whole again, say thank you. And instead of listening to those voices in your mind that are sowing dissent, telling you – *erroneously* – about what you're *owed*...instead look at what you've been *given*, and then just say thank you.

"I know this...time...seems dark...to you, but it's only because you're looking inward and you're afraid. It's so much easier to be angry than it is to be afraid. It's so much easier for us to say, 'No. Now. More.' than it is to say, 'Yes. Please. Thank you.' But, if the only prayer you ever say is thank you...that will be enough.'

"So, I ask you again, boss. What's it gonna be?"

David took a breath.

In that moment, he wanted to abandon his frustration and let Virgil's words resonate within him, let them fill him up. He wanted to allow long gestating tears to flow freely, to grieve all of the things he had lost in his life, and to release all of the tension knotted up inside of him.

Instead, he found himself simply nodding slightly. "You don't have to worry about me. That's all I meant. I'll be fine."

41

It felt like night. David was fairly sure it was night. He wondered then, for the first time, why the room had no clocks.

Probably to keep me from literally going insane watching the minutes drag.

The lights had been flickering off and on all afternoon. The wind was intense outside, ripping at the building. As much as David didn't like being in here, he couldn't even imagine being out there in the cold.

The hospital itself seemed asleep to him now.

Mr. Mahnung's bed remained empty. James hadn't returned, nor had Monica. Even Virgil hadn't come for physical therapy, although he had stopped in briefly to loan David his copy of a book: the collected writings of Meister Eckhart. David noticed right away that the pages of the book were dog-eared and frayed, yellowed by the sun; it had been well used.

David glanced at the book, even considered picking it up, but ultimately left it lying there on the rolling cart. Instead, he resorted to watching the tiny television. As he turned it on, the first movie he encountered was *Shock Corridor*, a Samuel Fuller film from the sixties. David felt like he had seen it in college and not enjoyed it much then. And, as it took place in a mental institution, he felt like it might be striking a little too close to home. Instead he flipped the dial again. Next up was *Ren and Stimpy*. He flipped away from the cartoon almost immediately; it made him think of Mr. Mahnung, and those weren't thoughts he welcomed. Finally he settled on an adaptation of *Burberry Place*, a novel he'd quite enjoyed. Although he could tell just from watching a few minutes of it that it wasn't going to do the book justice – bad acting, low production value – he figured he'd leave it on until he fell asleep.

Unfortunately, just as he started to get into it, the overhead lights and television fluttered out, replaced once again by the emergency lighting. The wind outside thundered on cue, as if to drive home the reason why.

David took a deep breath. He was bored and tired, but not sleepy. He wasn't interested in any more crossword puzzles. And he felt like he'd read nearly every magazine the hospital owned. He sighed again.

From his vantage point in bed, he could see straight down a long hallway that intersected the corridor outside of his room. He wondered if it was the same hallway he'd traveled down by way of gurney that first day in the hospital. *Was it the first day?* He didn't even know anymore.

It seemed darker to him now. Darker even than the dim half-light the emergency lighting allowed. And the more he stared into it, the darker it seemed to become. He blinked his eyes, tried to let them acclimate to the new lighting.

The hallway seemed longer too. Had he ever really studied it before?

The wind roared, shaking the boards on his window, even the windows themselves; it sounded like a beast attempting to tear its way inside. Aside from the storm, however, the hospital seemed almost…abandoned, vacant.

David stared again into the darkness of the hallway and heard the familiar giggle of a little girl. *Judgmental little bitch*, he thought, smiling to himself. And then there was another sound. A sound he was familiar with. The squeaking of a wheelchair, an older one, wheels badly in need of oil. Just like his mother's chair. His skin crawled at the sound.

The overhead lights fluttered to life for a brief moment and then went out again, shunting everything back to the emergency lighting. It was just a split second of light, a flash of illumination down the hallway, but David could have sworn he saw a figure in a wheelchair making its way toward him.

The squeal of the wheels continued.

Again he blinked and tried to peer into the darkness, made even more oppressive by the fleeting moment of light. He couldn't see anything at all. Again, the little girl giggled; he couldn't tell which direction the noises were coming from anymore. He felt his breathing quicken.

Just then, there was another flash of the overheads, another moment of brightness. Like a strobe light, it was brilliant one moment and then gone, replaced by the dim lighting that had come before, leaving confusing and hazy after images in its wake. And once again, David thought he'd seen it. A figure in a wheelchair – dark, almost silhouetted, head lolling to the side. It was coming closer to him now.

He peered again into the darkness, gripping the sheets, willing his eyes to do better. His heart rate was elevated. Tiny beads of sweat coated his forehead. He could hear the wheels turning, steadily drawing nearer and nearer.

The call button was next to him on the bed. He wanted to pick it up, but knew he couldn't. He couldn't continue to appear insane. Not even if he was.

The overhead lights flickered on and off once more, even more briefly than before. The person – *the woman?* – in the wheelchair was not far away from him now. He could feel his heartbeat thudding in his throat. The noise of the screeching wheels nearly pierced his ears now, toyed with his rationality. Ever closer. Never pausing.

He stared into the hallway and the darkness seemed to close in around him, like a physical presence. It was no mere dim corridor now, but a chasm, reaching out for him, black as pitch. And he watched as a figure emerged from the blackness, a familiar looking woman in a wheelchair.

His eyes snapped shut and he heard the word *"No"* escape his lips. "No, no, no, no, no." He held his eyes shut tight. Felt his stomach clench. The squeal of the tires had turned into a constant shrill whine. "No, no, no, NO, NO!"

He stopped talking and clenched his jaw. He didn't want to open his eyes. Didn't want to see what was coming his way. Or was it there already? Sitting next to him? Slumping toward him? Needing his attention? His embrace?

Fear shifted again to anger. He felt stupid, weak. A hostage to his own paranoia. He wouldn't have it.

"NO!" he cried, opening his eyes wide.

In front of him was...nothing.

The overhead lights had returned. The TV power was back, and the screen showed color-bars. The squeal of the tires had metamorphosed into a steady tone emanating from the television set.

David grabbed the remote quickly and shut the set off.

He was covered in perspiration. The sheets were soaked through. His jaw was shaking; it hurt from the tension. His breathing was loud, labored.

But there was nothing unusual there at all. Not in the room. And not in the hallway. The hospital itself was still silent, except for the sound of the merciless storm outside.

42

It was the first shower David had taken unassisted. He wasn't sure they'd even approve of him going it alone, but he felt like he needed it. The process actually went much better than he anticipated. He let the shower curtain pool over his thighs as he washed himself, which served the dual purpose of keeping his dressings dry *and* hiding his injury from view.

David felt renewed after the shower, as if some of the day's unpleasantness had been physically washed away. He removed the wet bandages from his right arm, stopping briefly to examine the bruises and scrapes. It was looking better overall, he thought, except for one nasty scratch on his forearm. He'd need to ask one of the nurses to take a look at it, maybe re-bandage it, make sure that it wasn't getting infected; that was the last thing he needed. Then he put on a fresh hospital gown and lumbered back into the room.

The overhead lights had remained operational for a while now, and the room seemed stark, the yellow walls dull. The emergency lighting added visual interest that the room didn't deserve. Under the normal fluorescents, it was simply a hospital room. And it was a room he had grown dreadfully tired of.

He decided to take a trip out instead of returning to bed. Virgil had skipped their PT that day due to all of the excitement and David missed the change of scenery. He wondered if anyone might be in the recreation room. It was so hard to gauge just how late it actually was; perhaps everyone else was already asleep.

David hobbled into the corridor, glancing sideways down the adjoining hallway, the one that had seemed so dark and long to him earlier. It was pedestrian now, a hallway just like any other, lit evenly – too evenly – by the overheads. An unoccupied gurney sat halfway down on the left. An old woman using a walker slowly made her way in the opposite direction.

David continued down the corridor. As he neared the recreation room, he could hear noise: the mingling of a television news report and music from the radio. As he approached the doorway, he saw that there were several people inside. The same old man who had been there the last time was sitting near the radio in his wheelchair, listening to the music: "God Bless the Child" by Ella Fitzgerald. A dark-haired woman wearing a hospital gown was sitting at the table by herself playing solitaire; she seemed focused, a bit of a scowl on her face. A third patient, a middle-aged man with short cropped blonde hair, sat lazily on the couch watching the news report.

The well-dressed news anchor on the television screen was mid-sentence: "…calling it the Storm of the Century, and there is still no end in sight. For more on the situation, we go live to Tina Takamura on scene. Tina?"

The scene then shifted to a young Asian woman in heavy snow gear. She was speaking into a microphone while the wind bit at her exposed face, and flurries of snow blew around her. David smiled to himself. He never understood why the news felt the need to put unfortunate reporters in the midst of natural disasters. It wasn't like the audience wasn't going to believe them. *Why would you lie to us about a snowstorm? We get it. It's snow.*

The old man saw David in the doorway and smiled his toothless smile, raising a thin trembling hand slightly to greet him. David nodded in return, debating whether to stay or continue his journey around the hospital corridors. The old man seemed friendly enough, but David hated the idea of his wheelchair. Just then the old man motioned to one of the chairs nearby, and David felt like he'd be hard pressed to leave after such an obvious invitation. He moved in to the room, eyeing the wheelchair as he went. As he approached the old man, he was careful to keep a chair between them, a barrier.

The old man reached up and removed the oxygen tube from his nose, letting it dangle just under his chin. "I'm Curtis," he said. The lack of teeth gave his words a mushy quality; Curtis sounded more like *Cuth-es.*

"David."

Curtis nodded then pointed to David's leg and arm. "What happened, fella?"

"A car wreck."

"Ohhhh." Curtis grimaced, his forehead wrinkling even more. In return, he pointed to his own oxygen tube. "I've got emphysema," he wheezed. "Don't ever smoke."

David smiled. "I don't. My...my father died of emphysema."

"It's a bitch," Curtis said. The word bitch came out as *bish.*

David nodded. He hoped Curtis didn't pursue the topic any further. He didn't really want to talk about his father. Or emphysema. And he liked that Curtis hadn't dwelled on David's injuries.

David turned absently and glanced at the television. They were still talking to poor Tina Takamura, who seemed to be rushing through her report, obviously anxious to cover her face and go back inside.

"Damn it!" the dark-haired woman barked abruptly, banging her fist down on the small table. "So close! This deck is fucking defective, I tell you!"

"Hey, hey," the man on the couch said, "language please. Some of us are trying to watch the news. And some of us don't give a shit about your game."

"Every day, it's the same," the woman said, rising from the table. "Just when I think I'm gonna win, no. Something always blocks me. I feel like I've been playing this stupid game forever. But can I win? No! Not one goddamn time!" She made a sort of snorting noise, then dropped the deck back on the table and limped out of the room. David watched her go.

"Don't worry about her," Curtis said to David. "She's grumpy. She's always grumpy. I don't think she's right in the head."

"Grumpy my ass," the blonde man said. "That chick's just a bitch."

Curtis looked to David, raising his eyebrows and shaking his head, as if to say *What are you gonna do?*

"What are you listening to?" David asked, attempting a segue to another subject.

"Ella," Curtis smiled. "Beautiful voice, don't you think?" The old man began singing along, poorly. David couldn't help but grin.

"Hey pops, c'mon!" the blonde man said brusquely, motioning to the television. "Can you keep it to a low roar? A singer, you are not."

David turned, opening his mouth to say something, but Curtis lifted his fingers up and wagged them back and forth, dismissing the blonde man's words. He wrinkled his nose, pursed his lips, and shook his head at David. "Too many grumpy people already," Curtis said. "I just want to listen to my music."

David nodded. "I understand. She has a beautiful voice."

"Music is the answer," the old man replied, smiling broadly, bearing his gums. His eyes squinted.

David chuckled. "What's the question?"

The old man laughed, a shallow wheezing laugh, but one that was truly genuine. "Doesn't matter."

David liked Curtis. He wondered if the old man truly needed the wheelchair or if he chose it. He wasn't going to ask.

Just then, another figure moved into the room. It was the nurse, Tammy. She was dressed in burgundy scrubs, carrying a brown lunch bag and a bottle of water. She moved to the table directly, sat down, and began riffling through her bag.

"Oh, she's a good lookin' one," Curtis said.

David just smiled in return, sneaking stealthy glances in Tammy's direction.

"Well...go," Curtis said, "I would if I were you, and if the other choice was the likes of me."

"Well...rain check on the conversation, then?" David asked.

"Of course." Curtis smiled.

David rose awkwardly and made his way toward the table, but Tammy didn't look up. "Hey there," he said in his best casual manner.

"Mister 509," Tammy said, still not looking his way. She took a big bite of what appeared to be a chicken salad sandwich.

"Mind if I...?" David asked, indicating the seat across from her.

"Nope."

He sat down as quickly and gracefully as he could, leaning his crutches against the chair next to him. "So, you eat in here, huh?"

"Not always," she said, still chewing. Finally she swallowed, looked at David and said, "I get tired of the same old scenery. Don't you?"

"You have no idea."

"You know, you beat that man pretty badly today, 509," she murmured. At first, David assumed she meant to take him to task. He began to prepare a defense, but then hesitated, seeing a wry smile begin to form at the corners of her mouth. "You're the talk of the hospital. Aren't you the dangerous one."

David didn't know how to respond. He fumbled for the right words. "Not…dangerous. I was…it was a mistake."

"Too bad," she said, and then winked at him.

That wink.

She was flirting again, he thought. He hadn't imagined it before. "Why? Do you like dangerous boys?" he asked. He knew the question – an overtly cheesy attempt at a line – would produce only one of two possible responses. Either she would laugh at him, leave him sitting there by himself, rejected. Or… she wouldn't.

Tammy sized him up. She wasn't laughing.

"You look freshly showered," she whispered. "Didn't need any help, I see. Or did you call somebody else?"

David didn't know where this was going. But he knew he was enjoying the cheeky back and forth, the rather overt flirtation. It made him feel real again. "I did it all by my lonesome."

"Too bad." She tossed the remainder of the sandwich – mostly just crusts – into the bag and took a sip from her water bottle. It reminded David of Dana the night they'd met, her sipping suggestively from her beer. He pushed the thought away.

Tammy rose, still looking at him, and then turned, tossed the sandwich bag and water into the garbage can, and began to walk out. *Well,* David thought, *it was fun while it lasted.* He watched the way her ass shifted underneath her scrub bottoms, found himself wondering about what type of underwear she was wearing.

154

Then Tammy stopped in the doorway and turned back to David. She looked first at him, then down the corridor, then gave him a little nod and disappeared into the hallway.

David knew that nod. He'd seen it before.

He grabbed his crutches and moved himself into an upright position as quickly as possible. He noticed Curtis grinning at him again, giving him a small wave of salutation. David smiled back and then moved toward the doorway, following Tammy out into the hall.

He glanced right and then left. He saw her. She was about twenty feet away, standing next to a slightly open door on the right side of the hallway. She was looking in his direction, waiting for him. When she saw that he had noticed her, she glided inside deliberately with an obvious swinging of her hips, and let the door close behind her.

David felt a pang of indecision. This type of tryst – if that's what this was actually leading to – was not a foreign situation to him. The moments, the women, blended together in his memory. Urgent, almost frantic, groping in nightclub bathrooms, the backseats of cabs, his living room floor; women of all shapes and persuasions; names he was too drunk or too uninterested to recall. This wasn't new territory.

But so much *was* different now. His leg. His confidence. His ability to be that person once again.

I can't help but wonder when your last truly happy memory was.

But he needed this.

Fuck the nurse. I'm here to tell you to fuck the nurse.

He deserved to lose himself in this moment.

What the fuck does any of it matter now?

He wanted this. He wanted her. He repeated the words in his mind.

Slowly, he shuffled down the corridor, opened the door labeled SUPPLIES, and disappeared inside.

43

"You're distant," Dana said.

It was the day of her younger brother Michael's graduation from Pepperdine University School of Law. The weather had been extremely warm that day. Even with the ocean breeze, it had sapped David's energy. And that was before having to navigate the minefield that was Dana's family. They'd all gone to dinner at Nobu, a Japanese restaurant on the Malibu coast, a party of eight. It was Dana's parents, whom David had met once before, her brother Michael, two grandparents, and an aunt.

He'd done his best to be gracious, charming, witty. He'd fielded many questions from Dana's grandmother and aunt, especially concerning his plans for Dana. And he'd begun to feel a bit anxious, suffocated. The noise level had become overwhelming, the temperature stifling; or was it just him? He'd loosened his tie and shirt collar.

It was perhaps no small coincidence that he'd noticed Dana's hand tremor just as her aunt said, "So you two seem to be getting serious. Are there wedding bells in the future?" The tremor had been almost imperceptible. She'd reached for the soy sauce, a simple gesture. Postural tremors, that's what the doctors had called them. No one else would've noticed, not if they hadn't been looking for them.

Her family had loved him. He'd put on the charm. He'd made the right moves, said the right things, laughed in the proper places. He was quite capable of being likable when it suited him.

"You're distant and I think I know why," Dana repeated as they drove home along the Pacific Coast Highway, the ocean on their right, a dark expanse reflecting a moonlit sky. "My aunt and my grandma really made you uncomfortable, didn't they?"

David was silent. He watched the road wind ahead of them, snaking along the rocky coastline.

"Well, don't let them spook you," she said, reaching into her purse for her Altoids tin. "They're just that way. I don't even *want* to be married. Not for a *very* long time, anyway. So don't think I'm the one putting thoughts into their heads. I should've warned you."

"Okay," David said.

"Anyway, thanks for coming today," Dana went on. "I think Michael appreciates you making the effort. I'm not sure that my dad really likes you, but he doesn't like anyone."

"He likes me just fine. He said he was going to email me about his friend's start-up."

"Oh," Dana said, slightly surprised. "Well, okay then. I guess dad's lightening up. By the way, holy crap, did you have any of his Yellowtail Sashimi? That was freakin' amazing."

"I think we should take time apart." The statement came out of nowhere. David's tone was even, unemotional.

Dana's mouth dropped open. "What?"

"I just think…"

"Is this about my family today?" Dana asked. "Are you really freaking out or something? Baby…"

"No, this is…I just think…I'm not sure if I'm ready for this kind of commitment. You're…I'm feeling kind of smothered by you."

Dana's face soured, her tongue pressed the inside of her cheek. "By me? Oh bullshit, David. That's such…that's such amazing bullshit!"

David was silent. He gripped the steering wheel of the Mercedes tightly with both hands.

"I have put *zero* pressure on you to do *anything*. Me spending the night at your house? Always your idea. Us becoming a couple? Your idea. Me bringing a toothbrush and some other things to your place? That was you too. You coming *today* even? You!

"I know *you*. And I know guys *like* you. I enjoy your company, David, and we got along in more ways than one, and that's cool. But I have *never* made any sort of demand on you or your time. I haven't even *mentioned* the *word* 'future.' So, if you're feeling smothered, or whatever the fuck you want to call it, that's on you. That's in *your* head. What kind of commitment do you even think –" Dana stopped talking suddenly, her facial expression shifting, eyes widening, eyebrows raising. She looked like the wind had been knocked out her.

David glanced over, then back at the road. "What?"

"You coward."

"What?"

"This isn't even about the relationship stuff is it? You *fucking* coward."

David said nothing, but peered at the road intently, his jaw set. He swallowed.

"You saw the tremor at dinner. I *know* you did. That's what this is about, isn't it? This is about you *liking* me, maybe even *loving* me in your own special fucked-up David kind of way, but not having the sack to be around when things get dicey. Well…shit. Shit."

"Dana, I…" David started, but then trailed off. The rest of his thought went unspoken.

"No, it's good. You can drop me at home," Dana said, slumping back against the leather seat. "I'm just glad I found out

159

now. I would hate to think that you might've allowed yourself to get any deeper into my life before you realized you didn't have the stones for something real. Because real is messy, David. It bleeds. It hurts. It doesn't always polish up to a pretty sheen.

"I really hope you learn that someday, but you know what? You're going to have to learn it on somebody else's dime."

44

The supply closet was dark, somewhat confined. David fumbled for a light switch.

"No lights," she whispered playfully. He could feel her hand on his. His eyes struggled to adjust to the dark. "Come here." Her voice was earthy, alluring. He could barely make out her outline in the dark. She was pulling her scrub top up over her head.

He shuffled toward her cautiously, wondering how this was ever going to work. He felt like half a man, unfit for the task at hand. Impotent.

Then suddenly, her lips were on his, her tongue exploring his mouth. Her teeth bit into his lower lip gently, and he sighed.

"I've been watching you," she whispered, her smooth cheek against his, her hot breath tickling his ear. "I had a feeling about you."

He put pressure on the crutches and kissed her back hard. He felt his erection pressing against the flimsy gown. It reassured him, gave him a strange boost of confidence. At least a part of him – an important part – *was* ready for this.

David shifted his weight on the crutches to his wounded right arm, ignoring the twinge of pain that shot up his forearm. He reached out with his left hand and touched her face, pulling her to him, his lips meeting hers. They were soft, full. She smelled of bubblegum, a girl's perfume.

Her hand lifted his gown and found his erection, stroking him.

His hand made its way to her right breast and cupped it, held it lightly, his fingers caressing her rigid nipple, tweaking it. She bit his lip again, pulling on it slightly with her teeth. He closed his eyes, dizzy.

The crutches wobbled under his unsteady weight. He wasn't assured enough of his abilities for this. He was worried he was going to end up on the floor in a heap. The thought bothered him on multiple levels.

"Well, this won't do at all," she said, as if she were reading his mind. "Here baby, sit here and let me do all the work."

Tammy pushed him back, snatching the crutches from him. David gasped as he teetered backward and then landed on a soft fabric bench. Almost immediately, her lips were on his again, her hands were in his hair. She moved up onto him and straddled him, kissing him hard, almost desperately. His leg throbbed, but it was a pain he could endure. She sat straight, arching her back, and pulled him to her chest. Her full breasts were on his face, soft skin against his stubble. He took one of her nipples into his mouth. His hands gripped her naked back, fingers splayed. He traced the muscles of her taut back, following the curve of her spine down to the waistband of her scrubs. He pulled the fabric of the pants away from her body and slipped his hands underneath, gripping her firm backside, pulling her to him.

She leapt off of him again in a jolt, disappearing into the darkness. David kept waiting for his eyes to adjust, but it was still hard for him to see anything. Then she was back, on him again, her scrub pants abandoned, the smoothness of her legs against his thighs. He reached down between her legs and pulled her panties aside, felt the heat of her. She was kissing him again, hard, almost too hard. Her passion teetered on violence.

"Easy, okay?" David whispered.

Tammy didn't seem to hear him. Or she chose not to. Her body writhed against his. Her kisses were almost an assault of lust, desire. Her tongue found his mouth and her mouth covered his, until he began to think he wouldn't be able to breathe. He started to feel confined.

Smothered?

She pulled his gown out of the way and found his cock, guiding it inside of her hastily. Her breathing was intense. Her body seemed to be in constant movement. David wished she would relent, if only for a moment. His leg was aching.

She began to move on top of him forcefully, him inside of her, her hips grating against him in rhythmic thrusts. David was having trouble finding pleasure in the act. It was simply too much.

"Can you...?"

"Can I what?" she hissed in his ear. Her voice was low and gravelly, full of hunger.

His hand gripped her waist, hoping to guide her, restrain her movement, but her skin felt different to him now. Not soft like before, but coarse. *Gooseflesh?* he wondered.

Her tongue snaked its way into his mouth again. And he realized that her breath was foul. He hadn't noticed it before. She tasted like a combination of stale chicken salad and cigarettes. And it wasn't just her breath, her whole body stank. Her flesh smelled like she hadn't showered in weeks. The scent wafted into the air from the constant undulation of her sinewy form. Her hips gyrated against him, chafing his flesh.

"Please..." he begged.

His hands moved up her back, gripping her flesh.

And then her skin began to rip away under his touch.

His fingers sank inside of her. His eyes shot open wide. Her body heaved unremittingly. In the darkness, he could see her face near his, her skin was gray and festering, her eyes were black pools.

David cried out and pushed her off of him with all of his force. The rotting thing that was once Tammy was flung back away into the darkness, out of view. He heard it land with a thud.

And then it sniggered in the gloom.

His heart raced. He leaned down, blindly searching the floor for his crutches. But they were nowhere to be found.

The thing laughed again in the darkness. "Awww, and I was having ssssoo much fun," it whispered.

David's hands moved desperately along the floor, his fingers moving frantically, hoping for any sign of his crutches. His heart thundered in his chest. He stared straight ahead into the darkness, searching for any movement. And then his fingers touched something. Metal. But not a crutch. A curve. Spokes.

The curve of a tire.

He felt the blood drain from his face and his breath hitch as a realization swept over him. He hadn't been sitting on a bench at all, he had been sitting in a wheelchair!

Just then, the thing came out of the darkness, cackling. It leaped onto him, straddling him again, pushing him down. Its flesh was hanging now, gelatinous, decaying, its breasts drooping away, its stomach riddled with sores. He could just make out its face, its hair frayed and wiry, its eyes bulging, the holes in the skin of its cheeks giving way to the rotting teeth and gums beneath.

"I thought you *liiiiked meeeee,*" it hissed, and came in as if to kiss him again. And as it did, its jaw dropped away, landing in David's lap. Its black tongue snaked out toward him. Its hands found their way into his hair, pulling him to it. And then its fingers began to break apart there, cracking and snapping, practically dissolving around his face.

David cried out again and went to push the thing off of him once more, but his hand sunk straight through its chest. He felt the somewhat dusty, somewhat viscous tissue melt around his arm as the thing began to liquefy on top of him, dissolving into nothing more than purulent fluid and tiny fragments of tissue and bone. It covered him.

David pulled at the sludge, scraping it away, continuing to scream.

He flung himself out of the chair, landing hard on the floor. He felt the pain shoot up his leg from the injury. His arm throbbed. His back ached.

What the hell just happened?! David's thoughts were jumbled, rapid. *What the fuck is going on?!*

The darkness was all around him now, darker than before, oppressive, closing in. He heard his own screams as if there were emanating from somewhere else.

And then he stopped. And took a breath.

David began to push the fear away, just as he always did. He could hear his exhalations reverberate in the blackness of the room, loud in his ears. He allowed himself to become calm, to slow his breathing, and he attempted to be still. He would *not* let this beat him.

How do you eat an elephant? he thought.

Slowly, methodically, he began to claw his way around the room, combing the floor with his one good hand, searching. Until finally, he felt something. A long cylinder of metal. His crutches. First one, and then the other, right nearby.

One bite at a time.

He'd never gotten up from the floor before like this, and now he'd have to do it without any light.

One bite at a time.

He went gradually, using a single crutch to pull himself up. And then he shifted his weight to the other. Until finally, he was upright again.

Now, he thought, *just to find the door.*

He was careful not to move back in the direction of the wheelchair, now covered in the remains of the thing that used to be Tammy. Slowly, carefully, he found a wall, then began to follow it around the room until he felt a smooth surface. And a handle. *The door.*

He went to turn the handle, relieved to escape this nightmare at last, but the door wouldn't budge. He groaned. It was locked from the outside.

Fuck.

His hands fumbled next to the door for a light switch, and David felt relieved when he found it. But even as he flipped each switch up and down, none of his movements produced light.

A slow realization crept over him. He was trapped there in that supply room. He was trapped there in the darkness.

45

David pounded on the door, shouting, trying not to let the weight of the room's darkness overwhelm him.

"Help! I'm stuck in here! Help me! Someone!"

He stopped and pressed his ear against the solid door; the side of his left hand was throbbing from striking it repeatedly. He could hear no movement out in the hallway. In the distance, he thought he could hear the noise of the recreation room, the drone of a television, perhaps? He wasn't certain. The silence of the dark room itself seemed to have a tone, a heaviness that pushed against his eardrums.

Just then, he thought he heard something moving behind him in the supply closet, a skittering of feet, a brushing against shelves.

David took a breath, and pushed the idea from his mind. *Madness,* he thought. *I'm going insane.*

He'd come into the room with another person, an attractive, vivacious human being, and that human being was gone now. He'd seen her – *felt her* – dissolve away into nothingness, a putrefied sludge. So, what did it all mean? Was he truly going crazy? Had he only ever come into the room alone? Had he only ever imagined James? Imagined the man screaming with no mouth? And Mr. Mahnung speaking to him? Or was there some other explanation? Some sinister explanation? Was it *this place?*

How could he be certain of anything?

"Hello!" He took up his pounding with renewed vigor, focusing on the only thing that could help him, ignoring any thoughts of waning sanity or malevolent entities, neither of which was helpful to him. Not now. Not here in the dark. "Hello!"

He stopped. There was a knock on the other side of the door. David recoiled, startled. He felt the crutches wobble in the dark. He didn't want to go to the floor again. That hadn't been a pleasant experience.

"Hello?" he said. "Can you hear me? I'm locked in!"

There was a chuckling on the other side of the door.

God help me, David thought.

"Hello?" he repeated.

"You," the voice responded, "were always so much better at this shit before. About not getting caught with your pants down."

It was James' voice. David sighed, relieved.

Relieved that it was only the dead guy.

"I don't have pants now," David said, attempting a joke. It felt wrong. He didn't want to joke. He wanted out of the darkness. But a part of him worried that James wouldn't let him out, that his friend, if not entertained, might wander away distracted, disappear as usual. David knocked again on his side of the door, rhythmically. *Shave and a hair cut...*

Two knocks came from the hall in return. *...two bits.*

"Can you let me out, James?" David asked quietly.

"Why?" James replied, flippantly.

David bit his tongue. *Don't piss him off, don't piss him off!* "Because I'm locked in here and the lights don't work. I can't see anything."

James laughed. "What's new?"

"C'mon, man!" David said, trying not to sound angry.

"If I let you out, then what?"

David shook his head. "Then what...what?"

There was a silence. David worried James was already gone.

"James?" he said, pounding on the door tentatively.

"What are you doing, David? How long are you going to do this?" James said. His voice sounded closer, right up against the door.

"James, please," David begged. He felt on the verge of hysteria. Or was he already long past that point? "James, it's not me…it's *this place.*"

"This place?" James echoed.

"Yes," David whimpered. "I think so."

There was another long silence.

"James!"

The silence continued. David opened his mouth to call out again, beginning to despair, when finally James said quietly, "You haven't changed."

The lock turned and the door opened slightly. The light felt like oxygen to David. The air in the closet suddenly seemed stale, noxious. He was anxious to be free of it.

David pushed the door open wider, and felt a weight lift off of him. He blinked his eyes as his pupils dilated. And as the hallway lights crept in, David turned back, anticipating that he would find Tammy's viscous remains sprayed on the walls, pooled on the floor, coating the wheelchair, coating him. But even in the dim light he could see that there was nothing there. No remains. No mucous, no detritus, no gore. It was just a normal, everyday supply closet. There were racks of shelves holding tubs, drawers, cabinets – *concealing what? medication* – a bucket and a mop, several crutches and walkers, and one lone wheelchair, recently cleaned and polished. Spotless.

David shuddered. *Madness.*

As he moved into the hallway, he saw that the generator power was on, the corridor lit by the emergency lights. He hadn't been able to see the shift in the dark closet.

James was nowhere to be seen. The hallway was barren.

The vividness of the closet was already fading in his memory. The pieces that remained hung disjointed, like the hazy remnants of a mostly forgotten dream.

As David started back toward his room, the sound of his crutches against the tile echoed through the deserted corridor. He couldn't help but feel that the life had been drained from the building while he was trapped away in the closet, as if he were now walking down the hallway of some empty movie set, and not a real working hospital at all; he imagined extras sitting in waiting areas, reading newspapers, snacking on donuts, ready to populate the halls again on cue.

The recreation room was dark, quiet. Obviously he hadn't heard the television, not if they'd been running on generator. As he hobbled past the doorway, he glanced in, and his eyes went to the radio to see if Curtis was sitting nearby. He wasn't. But his wheelchair was there, unattended. David began to assume that he'd answered his own question from earlier – had Curtis *needed* the chair or chosen it – when movement near the couches caught his eye. Two men. Orderlies, David assumed. He hadn't noticed them before. They were attending to something on the floor. David looked closer and saw that it was a body bag. One of them was zipping it up, concealing what – *who* – was inside.

The two men lifted the bag, moving it to a gurney nearby. Their movements were smooth, nearly soundless. The man nearest to David turned, and looked at him; the man's face was expressionless, impassive.

The men moved the gurney out into the hall past David. Still, their movements seemed muted, nearly noiseless: the gurney wheels turning, running across the tiled floor, their footfalls. They moved past David wordlessly, and turned down the hallway that intersected near Room 509.

David limped after them, more in the direction of his room than actually following behind. He hoped it wasn't Curtis. He'd liked the old man, and hoped to continue visiting with him, felt like there was more to say.

Rain check?

As David neared his room he glanced down the adjoining hallway just as the men entered the service elevator, pulling the gurney in behind them.

The one and only floor, unless you count the basement.

As the elevator doors slid shut silently, David thought he saw one of the men nod to him. It was a slight, almost imperceptible gesture. And then they were both gone.

Gone. To the basement.

David shuddered at the thought of it, not really understanding why. He hadn't really even known Curtis. Maybe it wasn't even the old man in the bag. Still, something about all of it seemed final.

Unless you count the basement, which I do not.

He took one more glance at the elevator doors and then moved into his room.

46

In the bathroom, David ran the water, splashing it onto his face. It was cool. It felt good to him. His whole body ached. His leg, his arm. Even his face felt hot. He'd made a huge mistake going into the supply closet. Whether the experience itself had been real or imagined, he'd made a mistake going in. His judgment was suspect.

He wondered how to proceed now. Would he tell them about the things he'd been experiencing? Would he tell Virgil and Dr. Devar, throw himself on their mercy? Perhaps he truly *needed* mental help. Perhaps the shock of the accident – of losing a limb, losing his best friend – had all just been too much.

We're Graces. We don't quit.

No. They didn't. *He* didn't. David had never quit anything. Had never surrendered. Never hoisted the white flag. No, he'd kept his head down and kept moving forward his entire life, like a shark, leaving the others – the detractors and naysayers – in his wake. And he'd always come out on top. He could do this too.

"Oww!" he said suddenly as a violent pain shot up his right arm. He really *had* overexerted himself. He'd definitely need to have that arm looked at. And then what? What if they could tell he'd been out, that he'd fallen down. How could he explain… "Fuck!" he said, grabbing his arm, holding it tightly. Suddenly, the pain was intense. He blew air out of his lungs.

Ride it out, he thought.

A dark spot of red appeared in the sink. A tiny splatter. And then another.

David was bewildered at first. His brow creased. He looked up, half expecting there to be a leak in the ceiling. But then realized how silly that thought was. He was leaning over the sink, blocking it. Whatever it was *had* to be coming from him.

He pulled his hand away and watched as blood tickled down his right arm, dripping into the sink. One new spot. And then two more. Drip, drip, drip.

What the hell?

David grabbed at his arm, raising it up toward his face. He'd done this many times before despite his injuries, but now as he lifted his right arm, turned it, the pain seized him.

Mother of God.

His arm was on fire. It felt like it was tearing in two. Another deep breath. He rode out a wave of pain.

Once it had passed, he lifted his arm again slowly, bringing it closer to his face, exposing the flesh of his forearm. In the center was the cut he'd been concerned about before. Now it was inflamed, puffy. The wound ran from near his wrist along the soft underside of his forearm, following his veins and tendons. Along the center, it had reopened, and it was white along the edges. It was very clearly infected, blood seeping from the inflamed slit.

How had it gotten so bad since just this morning, he wondered. *Was* it just this morning? Or this afternoon? It hadn't been long at all…had it?

If only he hadn't gone into the closet. He knew that he'd made things so much worse by going. He should call the nurse. He knew that he should. But he wasn't ready to face them. Not just yet. He knew there had to be something around there to sterilize it with. His eyes raced around the small bathroom and settled on the disinfectant wipes near the toilet. He hobbled over to them. Even putting his weight on the crutches sent jolts of agony shooting down his right arm now.

Small drops of blood speckled the tile floor.

David lowered himself and sat cautiously on the edge of the toilet, holding his right arm in the air flat, palm turned up. Blood had pooled in the cut. He looked at it again. It seemed even worse in this new light. There were pockets of pus along the edges of the wound, red streaking on the skin of his arm.

He grabbed one of the disinfectant wipes with his left hand, careful to keep his right arm flat, and tore the edge off the package with his teeth. He pulled the wipe out and floated it over the wound. It seemed almost silly now. The wound seemed so much worse than before.

How had this happened, he thought? Out of nowhere.

He pressed the wipe down on top of the cut, applying slight pressure. Immediately, pus oozed out. David clamped his teeth down, hissing under the stinging pain. The wound was warm to the touch, hot even. He patted the wipe along its length, tensing as he went. So much pain he thought he might pass out. The wipe was saturated in blood and discharge in no time. He could smell the wound now; it was like rotting meat. He felt like he might be sick.

He tossed the wipe toward the sink, but missed. It hit the edge of the cabinet and slid down to the floor slowly. A problem for later, he figured. His fingers found the roll of toilet paper nearby and he pulled, wadding up a thick ball of tissue. Then, gently, he began to pat the length of the cut. More stabbing pain.

Dear God!

Why did it feel even wider to him now? Was it because he had drained some of the pus? Abated the inflammation with the disinfectant? Had the mouth of the wound retreated?

This time, he tossed the wad of tissues, now a soppy red pulp, toward the trash instead of the sink, and didn't miss.

One more disinfectant wipe, he thought, *and then I'll call the nurse.* He grabbed another, still elevating his wrist, and tore it open with his teeth. The stabbing pain through his arm hadn't lessened, and he knew the disinfectant would still sting. He took another deep breath and braced himself. He began to lower the wipe onto the cut when he noticed something there: a greyish white worm-like stub in the midst of his open wound, the width of a pencil. He tilted his head, moving closer to it. Had it been there all along? Had he just revealed it now that the inflammation was subsiding? And what was it that he was seeing?

David moved his arm higher, bringing it nearer to his face. He palmed the wipe in his left hand, and extended a finger, bringing it softly down toward the stub.

He stiffened, expecting pain, but he didn't need to. Before his finger could make contact, the stub disappeared, withdrawing inside of him quickly. David jumped. He felt his skin creep.

A parasite? he wondered. *I have a parasite? Inside of me?!*

He was shaking. He raised his arm up again, getting as close to it as he felt comfortable, and he watched, eyes squinted. It turned his stomach to realize that it was moving. Under his flesh. Burrowing in his wound, moving along under the surface of his skin. He felt a combination of nausea and dizziness wash over him. He felt faint.

Dear Lord.

His heart was racing. His forehead was saturated by perspiration.

It's this thing, he thought. *This THING is responsible. For the visions. The insane notions. This thing is to blame! I'm… I'm infected!*

David felt himself becoming angry, almost frantically so.

And then the worm reappeared, popping its thin ashen head out of the wound like a periscope. It wriggled to the surface and held there, coated in a sheen of blood.

David watched it reemerge and felt his blood boil at the sight of it sitting there, bathing in his fluids, subsisting off of him most likely. It was *mocking* him. He felt an impulse bubble up within him, and without warning, he thrust his fingers into the wound, grasping the head of the worm. He winced in agony, heard himself cry out, and felt the thing writhing beneath his flesh, struggling to pull away from him and disappear again. But he wouldn't let go.

Instead, he gritted his teeth and slowly began to pull the creature from his body, inch by nauseating inch.

47

"David! Oh my God!" the voice cried out from behind him in the bathroom doorway. It was Monica.

David turned to her, holding the worm firmly. He was glad she was here to bear witness to what was taking place. To see firsthand what had been driving him to such extremes, this *thing* living inside of his skin. It was nearly six inches long and still fighting him.

Monica was ashen, her mouth agape. Her eyes were fixated on his arm. She turned quickly, leaned out of the bathroom, and yelled, "Security! I need security!"

Security? Why? David figured she needed a doctor – a surgeon – and quickly.

When she turned back to him, she was shaking her head. She held up her hands in front of her body, fingers up, palms out. "You're going to be okay," she said, her voice soft and trembling. "You need to let me take care of you."

"That's fine," David said, then added, "I've never seen anything like this before, have you? What the hell is it?"

"David," she said, inching toward him. "You need to put it down."

What? Why?

"Are you crazy?" he asked. "It'll get away."

He heard the sounds of footsteps heading their way, heavy ones.

"David, just put it down," she urged. "So that we can help you."

David shook his head. He couldn't comprehend. Why would she want it to get away? Why wouldn't she want to help him? To help him pull it out? He felt a sudden swell of dizziness.

Fever. He knew that he'd lost blood, but not that much. It couldn't possibly have been that much.

Two men appeared in the doorway, orderlies. The taller of the two recoiled in horror at the sight of David, and he retched. David understood the feeling.

"Please," Monica begged, "please just put it down. Don't you see what you're doing to yourself, David? Can't you see?"

See? he thought, *of course I can see.* He wondered if he were the only one.

"I need…to get it out," David said, gritting his teeth.

Monica shook her head decisively. "No. You need to stop. You need to let go, and put the knife down so that we can help you?"

Knife? What?

David scoffed aloud, his nose wrinkled up.

The two men in the doorway slowly started to fall in behind Monica. But with one hand she motioned for them to keep their distance. She maintained her eye contact with David.

"David, look," she said. "Look at what you're doing to yourself. Just look at it."

David did. He looked down. And he felt the breath hold in his lungs, felt a twisting in his gut, felt his world freeze.

Nothing was the same.

The smattering of blood on the floor was now a puddle of crimson red, brilliant against the white bathroom tile, soaking the bath mat, pooling around his naked toes. The disinfectant wipe in his palm was now a blade, a sharpened kitchen knife; where had it even come from? But worst of all, the thing that made him want to drop to his knees in utter repulsion, was the worm. Because it wasn't a worm at all. It was his own tendon, ripped free of its home beneath his skin, a pale, wiry length of fibrous tissue torn from the uneven, festering gash that ran the length of his arm. His fingers were wrapped around the severed end, holding it tightly, pulling it from his flesh.

The realization overwhelmed him. The pain suddenly manifested. He felt his body start to collapse, heard the knife drop to the tile, then saw the image of Monica and the other men twist in his vision and invert as his head connected with the hard floor.

48

Where was he?

It was fuzzy in his head, hard to think. David tried to blink, but his eyelids were like weights.

Cinch it tight. Don't want wriggling.

His breathing was shallow. He heard the beeping of the machine. He was thirsty. His tongue was dry.

Oh my God. What the hell did he do?

He felt a warmth flowing through his veins. It was nice. Different than the chill on his feverish skin, the dampness of the sheets. He tried to smile, but wasn't sure if he succeeded or not. He glanced down at the length of his body. Images of the room stacked up on top of one another at odd angles like half transparent snapshots. David raised his eyebrows, but the movement hurt his head. He blinked again.

Where did this infection come from? How could it have spread so quickly?

There was a strap across his chest, another at his waist, and one more across his upper thighs. His left hand and leg were both bound by leather straps. He tried to test one but realized he had no strength to do so. Bodies moved around him in the room, but they appeared as no more than streaks, the afterimage of a shaky camera.

I'm not sure if we can save this.

There was something in the background, behind the beeping of the machine, underneath the sporadic noise of the room. A tune. One that he knew. *Moonlight Sonata, my old friend.*

But more than that. There were voices. A chant. Little girl voices. Laid over the top of Beethoven in juxtaposition.

Ice cream, soda pop, cherry on top,
Who's your boyfriend, I forgot;
Goes A...B...C...D...E...

So familiar. Where was that from?

He shook his head slightly; it was an insignificant motion that felt like violence inside his skull.

Little girls. Playground noises. The noise of a rope on pavement.

Fudge, fudge, tell the judge, momma's got a baby!
It isn't a boy, it isn't a girl, it's just a little lady!
A...B...C...

David knew. It was his elementary school. Right after his mother had been hit by the car. He was ten then. The little girls had liked to play jump-rope in the courtyard. The other boys and girls had been off on the soccer field, tetherball courts, or swing sets.

David would sit by the brown brick columns supporting the overhang by the cafeteria, keeping to himself, eating the snack from his sack lunch. And he'd listen to the nearby girls chanting nonsensical rhymes as they endeavored to beat previous records. And *he'd* count the minutes – the seconds – until he could just go back inside and concentrate on his studies. And forget to remember for a little while.

It was the one little girl who'd begun to tease him. She was the leader of the group. What was her name? He couldn't even recall anymore. She had been a nasty one, that little girl. A freckled blonde with a gap in her teeth and a frown on her face. Always a frown. Everyone had always ignored him hanging out there until the day she'd decided to make him a target.

He remembered her clearly on that day. That day she'd stopped jump-roping and come his way. She had been wearing her hair in pigtails, had been dressed in ruffles. She was a cruel but popular little thing, and the other jump rope girls had followed her lead.

"Hey, you," she said. "You're the one whose mommy's in a wheelchair!" She had said it so casually, pointing at him. Her voice had been louder than he would've liked, and she had drawn the attention of the others. "What happened to her? What happened to your mommy?"

David hadn't responded. He'd simply sat there motionless, somewhat surprised that she had been speaking to him. That she had mentioned his mother. He had never really thought of other people talking about his mother.

"I heard…that sshe wass a prossssstitute!" she'd said, lisping. "I heard ssshe got hit because she was on the sssstreet corner!" The other girls had gathered around her now, and they were giggling.

David had just shaken his head, trying to ignore her, hoping that she'd grow bored and wander away. But no.

"Isss that true? Isss it?" she'd continued to goad him.

David picked up his lunch and turned to leave when she'd started the chant.

"Mama's in a wheelchair! Mama's in a wheelchair! Mama's in a wheelchair!"

The others had joined in with her then. And it had felt like a wall of sound. As if the entire school was there in that courtyard, pointing at him, leering, mocking him. He knew now, looking back, that such a thing wasn't possible. It had only been a handful of unkind ten-year-old girls, momentarily diverted from playing jump rope. Still, he'd never gone into the courtyard during break time again. He'd located other hiding places where he could count the moments until break was over, until school was over, until it was time to take care of *her* again.

The memory faded away. But as his eyes closed, the chanting remained.

> *Down in the valley where the green grass grows,*
> *There sat Janey sweet as a rose.*
> *Along came Johnny and kissed her on the cheek.*
> *How many kisses did she get this week?*
> *A...B...C...D...E...F...*

He felt his gurney begin to move. Wobbly. Tires squeaking. He opened his eyes and, for a moment, he thought he glimpsed her. The little girl with the gap teeth. The girl whose name he'd forgotten. But when he blinked again, she was gone, relegated to his memories once more.

The gurney moved along steadily and, as it went, he felt himself sink back under familiar waves of murk, a coarse, but temporary darkness.

49

David awoke in a panic, confused. The room was dark. *The generator again?* he wondered. More than that though, it was different now. All of the lights were out in Room 509. No lighting spilled in from the hall. And none of the normal daylight snuck through the boards on the windows. There was just enough ambient light for him to know where he was; he'd become accustomed to seeing the ceiling this way, and knew it was his room, his bed.

He tried to move his head but couldn't; a leather strap across his forehead held him firmly in place against the pillows. His range of motion was limited to just the ceiling above.

His right arm throbbed. Hoping to examine it, he attempted to lift it into the air, but found that both his body and arms were restrained as well. A shot of adrenaline coursed through him. His eyes opened wide. He gritted his teeth, feeling suddenly claustrophobic. Caged. Like an animal.

David listened. He heard a fly buzz in the stillness of his room, unseen. There was laughter in the hallway, a low chuckle. Was someone in the doorway? Watching him? Was he a joke to someone?

"Who's there?" he said loudly. His voice was hoarse again, his throat raw. Had he been intubated again? How long had he been out? *How long have I been here now?*

There was no response. The person standing in the hallway simply chuckled again.

"Who are you? What do you want?" David asked. His voice sounded feeble.

The laughter dissipated along with the shuffling of footsteps as the person moved away down the corridor, leaving David alone again with the quiet. He listened to himself breathing, to the fly buzzing sporadically in short bursts, to the very stillness of the air itself.

And then there was something else. It was far off. Down the hall, he assumed. But it was a noise he was well familiar with, one he hoped never to hear again: the squealing of wheelchair wheels badly in need of lubricant. The noise was drawing closer.

David felt his body tense at the sound, his breathing hasten. He struggled to move his head, to be free of the restrictions, but to no avail. He was weak and they were tight.

The wheelchair was coming closer. Squeaking. Squealing. A chorus of monotonous noise, raw steel passing steel. Slowing turning wheels, hand-powered.

David heard his father's words again. They echoed in his mind: *We don't quit. Now get up, and get dressed.*

He wanted to. So, so desperately. He wanted to leave this place behind, and never look back at it. It had taken too much of him already.

The noise of the tires was moving closer.

You haven't changed.

But he had. So much. He'd sacrificed so much of himself for so long. The thought of it temporarily replaced his fear with a simmering anger, a bitterness. For a moment he was able to visualize the approaching wheelchair, old and in need of maintenance, driven by the twisted fingers of the sick and broken, the deformed and the defective. He imagined disposing of it, heaving it from the top of a cliff, listening to it fall, crash, twist. An explosion of metal.

Like a car crash.

The turning of the wheels drew ever closer. It was just outside in the hall now, he was sure of it.

None of it's real, buddy. Those were James' words. David wished he could believe them now. Wished he could believe that he could close his eyes and fall away from this nightmare. Wake to the real world once again.

Squeak. Squeak. Was it right outside his room now? Entering the doorway? It was so close. David wished he could turn his head. It might be better to see what was coming.

The squealing noise was loud now. It was definitely in the room with him. Coming closer to him. He felt his jaw quaver.

And then it stopped.

It was next to him.

His heart was beating so hard he wondered if it might explode out of his chest. He opened his mouth as if to speak, but no words came forth.

Silence.

But he could feel a presence in the room. It was nearby.

He waited. He wished whoever it was would either have their say or leave him be. His body was tense. His arm ached. His breaths came in abrupt spasms; the noise was the only thing he could hear.

And then he felt it. A touch on his left arm. Clammy against his feverish skin. He felt his flesh crawl.

"Daaaaaaavid," the voice rasped out. It was a moan most familiar to his ears.

He said nothing. He stared straight ahead at the ceiling, his only view, and felt tears of panic come into his eyes.

The touch moved up his arm, patting him slightly, awkwardly. "Daaaavid."

It was too much. His heart was a jackhammer. His breathing was too fast, shallow gasps. His eyes rolled back in his head, and David fainted away.

186

PART VII:
THE WHITE

50

"Daaavid," the word came deep, labored, full of pain.

He heard it as if from a distance, reverberating in the darkness, faint.

"Daaaaaviiiid." Again, but closer this time, pushed forth with great effort.

He felt himself being pulled from a deep and murky sleep, retreating from nightmares that, even then, he was unable to recall. He could feel the coolness of the pillow under his head. The sluggishness of his blood. And the rough skin against his forearm, a tender but terrifying touch.

David kept his eyes shut tight, afraid of what he might see when he opened them, afraid that the stark reality might match his deepest fears.

"Daaavid."

No. He didn't want to see.

"David, wake up." The voice was pleasant now, younger sounding, vibrant, wrapped in a smile. "Don't you want to ride, silly?"

His eyes flew open. He was filled with excitement. Today, he would ride his bike at last. With her help, he would do it. The training wheels would come off and he would ride.

David was six years old.

His mother sat on the edge of his bed, rubbing his arm gently. She was smiling at him, beautiful in her striped pullover, which hung off one shoulder. Her long, disheveled dirty-blonde hair framed her face. Her cherubic cheeks were out of place on a face so thin. Her hazel eyes were soft, hooded, wrinkled at the edges. Too much smiling, she'd always said.

Never.

David was wide awake at the thought of riding. He hugged her tightly, squashing his face into her chest; the tiny gold cross she always wore around her neck pressed against his cheek leaving an imprint.

"Will you help me?" he asked. He knew the answer. He wanted her to say it again.

"Yes, my little amazing. I will *always.*"

He could barely contain his smile. He'd been so frustrated with previous attempts at riding on his own. His father had tried to help David but had always been too impatient with him; David would get flustered and then he would fall. Always, after an exasperating hour or so, the training wheels had gone back on. But today, with his mother behind him, he would conquer this challenge. He had no doubt. He was excited to join his friends at play, grown up and riding all on his own.

He got dressed fast and met her downstairs. She fixed him cereal: Apple Jacks, his favorite. She served it to him in his grandmother's stainless steel bowl, the one that always kept the milk really cold. And then they went outside.

There was something reassuring about her being there behind him. He knew she wouldn't let him fall, wouldn't get frustrated by him. They could do this.

For the first hour, it wasn't working. His mother remained steady, full of praise, telling him how close he had come, all the things he was doing right.

David became discouraged, regardless of her approval.

"I'll just keep the training wheels," he said.

"Now, what would that look like? You're already such a little man. You don't *really* want to be the only one on training wheels, do you?" she asked, large plastic sunglasses perched on her nose, blonde hair swaying in the mid-summer breeze.

No, he most certainly didn't want to be the only one.

And so he'd recommitted.

"Go slowly. And don't think about me holding you," she instructed, her hands on the back of his bicycle seat. David's toes could barely reach the ground when parked. "You just have fun and don't be so serious. I'm here. I got you."

David set off again, determined. He tried to forget that she was there although that was almost impossible; her presence made it all so safe.

One foot around. And then the other. The wheels began to turn again. He felt her hands steady the wavering bicycle. He kept the handlebars stable, and focused.

"I got you, David. I got you."

Slowly at first. Slowly. And then a bit faster. He looked ahead, concentrated on his destination. Became unaware of the ground moving beneath him. And then, suddenly, everything locked into place, and the bicycle began moving more steadily.

"You're doing it!" she cried. "It's all you."

It's all you?

He glanced back and saw that the bicycle was pulling away from her, rocketing forward under his own power. Her form got smaller as he sped away, leaving her standing in the street, arms overhead, shrieking with joy.

His cheeks hurt from smiling. The wind whipped at his face, messed his hair. His feet went round, faster still. *He* was the pilot of this vehicle, the captain. Where once, just moments before, he couldn't, now suddenly he could. He could hear his mother shouting and whooping. He wondered if it would bring the neighbors into the street. He hoped so. He wanted them all to see.

He'd done it. With her there to hold him up, to support him, to love him. He'd done it.

And he wanted the moment to last forever.

51

His eyes shot open.

She wasn't there in the room with him. Not now. Not anymore. He still couldn't turn his head but he knew. She wasn't there now, if she ever was. The memory of her, young and vibrant, ached inside of him. But already, it was dissolving away like cotton candy on his tongue. And it made him miss her all over again.

The room wasn't so dark now. He could tell that it was daytime. And from what he could see, the generator power was on. He wished he could move his head.

He reached up with his left hand to scratch his face, but he'd forgotten that it was restrained. And where was his right hand now? Restrained as well?

No.

No, he didn't think so. He felt sick.

He heard someone enter the room. He tilted his head as much as possible to see who it was.

"Good morning, Mr. Grace," the voice said. Feminine, familiar. And then Dr. Devar came into his view.

"What happened?" David grunted. "What's going on? My throat…it hurts."

"Yes, that's normal. You were intubated. But it should go away in a little bit. Drink a bit of water, not too much. And chew on ice chips."

He blinked, confused. The room tilted a bit and he realized he was drugged again.

"How do I…?" he said, wiggling a bit under his restraints.

"Hopefully, we'll get those off of you soon. You were pretty delusional when they brought you in. We were worried about your safety."

"Brought me...I don't understand..." he sputtered.

"I'm Dr. Devar. I operated on you when you were brought in yesterday. What do you remember?"

What?!

"Brought in...I know...I've been here..."

Cauterize.

"I'm afraid you had an accident. Your car went off the side of an embankment into the snow. You were...very lucky to be found, actually."

"That was...weeks ago....I've been here....What's going on?!"

He was so tired of being confused.

The softness of her features transitioned into solemnity. "I have some bad news, David. Your friend died instantly in the crash. There was nothing anyone could do."

"What are you talking about!?" David shouted. Raising his voice hurt him.

She didn't seem to hear it. She continued as if on automatic pilot, a recording, an echo. And that's when he saw it. A subtle shifting under the skin on her face, a rolling of the tissue as if something was underneath, as if her face itself...was just a mask.

He felt the adrenaline course through him, layered on top of numerous other medications. He felt panicked and tired, all at the same time. He struggled to keep his eyes open.

"David, I need you to prepare yourself. You nearly died in that crash as well. Your vehicle rolled, and your right arm and right leg were trapped underneath. They were crushed, David. I'm very sorry to say that we tried, but we weren't able to save them."

She waited for him to react. David realized that she wasn't lying to him, he hadn't dreamed it. His arm was gone too. He knew that it was. They were taking him apart, piece by piece.

As she stared at him with a blank expression on her face, he felt a rage boil up within him.

"WHAT ARE YOU PEOPLE DOING TO ME?!" he screamed, his body writhing and convulsing under the restraints. "WHAT DO YOU WANT FROM ME?!"

He gritted his teeth, felt his body twitch.

She simply stared at him, seemingly unfazed by the outburst.

"I'm very sorry," she continued. "I know how shocking this all must be. But believe me when I tell you that you're very lucky just to be alive. Often in accidents like this…"

"GET AWAY FROM ME!!" he yelled. "WHAT ARE YOU?!"

He saw it again then: the rolling under her skin. And he knew. This wasn't a human being at all. This was a thing. A creature. Just like Tammy had been a creature. They were there to harm him. And he knew then that he must get away from this place. He must escape. Before there was nothing left of him at all.

"It's going to be okay," Dr. Devar said mechanically. "Take your time, David. I'll be here when you're ready to talk. I put a wheelchair here for you, for when we get those restraints off and get you moving."

She smiled at him, the approximation of a smile. Her once lovely dark eyes seemed dead to David. She turned and moved away from him, out of his field of view.

"Oh, and David," she whispered, "if you need anything…"

She didn't finish her thought. David didn't hear her leave. A part of him wondered if she hadn't. If perhaps she'd stayed there in the room, just out of sight, watching him.

After a few minutes, the effects of the drugs were too much. He couldn't keep his eyes open anymore. And as his eyelids slid shut, he thought he heard the sound of someone laughing.

52

Crying! Was someone crying? Sobs had filled the room, mournful. He was sure of it. His eyes flew open. He was disoriented, confused. It was the drugs, he was sure. Had someone been crying? Everything was jumbled.

His heart was racing, his breathing labored. He'd woken up from a dream, filled with panic, to find the regular hospital overhead lights back online. He was still restrained. And thirsty. His throat ached.

"Who is it?" he rasped. "Who's there?" His voice was grating, low.

"It's just me, hon." It was a female voice. Monica.

The memory of his strange interaction with Dr. Devar came back into his mind, and he wondered how long he'd been asleep this time.

"How...how long...?" he panted.

Monica came into his field of view, looking down at him. "How long what?" she asked, smiling politely.

"How long...have I been...here?" Every word pained him.

She looked confused. "Don't worry, not long."

"How...long?"

"I don't know..."

He swallowed hard; it felt like razor blades in gravel.

"I...didn't...I didn't come in...yesterday, right?" His tone, while stilted, was urgent. And he realized that he didn't know what to believe anymore. He wanted desperately to have something, anything that felt real. Something to believe in.

Monica frowned and paused, seemingly puzzled by his question.

"Monica!" he snapped. The one word was excruciating.

"No!" she yelped. "No, David…of course not."

He could see the fear in her again, fear of him. Of the monster she'd seen him be.

"And…my…my arm?" he asked, dropping his voice to a whisper.

She nodded solemnly, her eyes wide. She looked away from his face. "They had to…they had to amputate. You…you tore yourself to pieces."

So, it was true. That part of it anyway. He hadn't really been able to process it, not yet. Nothing about any of it seemed real. Dr. Devar and her creepy behavior might have simply been a drug-induced nightmare. But he was having trouble separating where dreams and reality split.

I really have gone insane.

"Can I…can I have…water?" he asked her, his voice stilted.

She nodded, then leaned in and loosened the leather restraint on his head. He grimaced under the lack of pressure and immediately felt his head begin to throb. Monica filled a paper cup with water from the pitcher on the rolling cart and tilted it to David's lips. He lifted his head to meet her, and as he did, he glanced down his body, still hidden under the blanket, strapped to the hospital bed; there was definitely less of him than there had been before.

He took small sips. The water felt alternatingly pleasing and then agonizing as it slid down his bruised throat. With each swallow, he expected to feel the pain subside, but it did not.

He glanced at the ceiling, the overhead lighting, a view he'd become accustomed to, and had a thought. Were the overhead lights indicative of his reality? Were they the dividing line between truth and hallucination? Now that the overheads were on, was he safe? Was it only the emergency lighting that was to fear? The thought gave him the slightest ray of hope. Perhaps if he could identify a common denominator, a root, then he could fix the problem.

"You don't want to overdo it," Monica said. "Not too much." She began to pull the cup away from his lips.

"Just…a little…more," David gulped.

"A little," she replied, smiling.

But as she tilted the cup back down to meet his waiting lips, David glanced movement under the skin of her hand. He saw it out of the corner of his eye, just a slight quiver.

Postural tremors?

He glanced up into Monica's face and she smiled at him again, disingenuously; it was the look of a person doing their very best to be pleasant despite circumstances. And then, as he looked back at her hand holding the cup, he saw it again, more directly this time: the skin on the back of her hand rippled up and then abated, like something adjusting itself under ill-fitting clothes.

53

The snowstorm outside was as bad as he'd heard it, raking against the boards on the windows, pushing the building itself around on its foundation.

As far as David could tell, the regular hospital lights were still on, although his room was dark. Not that it mattered, anyway. He'd seen what he'd seen, and that had happened with the lights on. So much for one theory. Still, he preferred it when the regular lights were active, when the hospital was flat and dull. Sterile.

A large gust of wind outside tore at the building.

Only a matter of time, he figured, *until the generator kicks in.*

He listened. At first, he thought he could hear voices down the hall, distant sounds of televisions, perhaps, ambience. But slowly, all noise faded away to the point where he assumed that he'd only imagined it. It was replaced instead by a dull tone, almost inaudible at first under the sounds of the snowstorm. It was deep and ponderous, a sound only audible when most other sounds had faded away; it felt imposing.

And then something else. A familiar girlish giggle.

He lifted his head up as much as he could, glad that Monica had left off the restraint, and he glanced around the dimness of his room, and into the hallway. Nothing there that he could see.

"David." It was a whisper, to his right. He turned but could see nothing. "David." From his left this time, he whipped his head around. Nothing.

Again, from the hallway came the girlish giggle.

"Leave me alone," he said aloud, surprised at his own voice.

"What happened to her?" the whisper said. It came from the end of the bed. It was androgynous, low-voiced and hushed. He glanced down the length of his body, peering past the edge of his bed into the darkness of the wall beyond. He could see nothing there.

And then another whisper, right next to his right ear: "What happened?"

He whipped his head around hard, pulling a muscle in his neck. But there was nothing.

Then he felt icy fingertips tracing along his right forearm, his brand new phantom limb. It sent a shiver up his spine to the base of his skull. He glanced down at the blanket where his arm used to be, and saw it moving, crumpling under an unseen touch. He could feel the cold fingers wrapping around his non-existent wrist, holding him.

"Break the shell." The whisper came again. And then once more, there was giggling in the hall.

"Leave me be," David whispered, closing his eyes. "Just leave me alone."

"You're already alone…" The voice seemed right in front of him now. He could almost feel hot breath on his face. He kept his eyes closed, felt his heart race. Rapid inhalations.

And then the cold hand released his wrist. And the tone disappeared. And all at once, the air went out of the room.

David opened his eyes carefully to the darkness.

He *was* alone.

54

"You…are falling apart faster than I am."

The voice woke David from a shallow sleep. It was James.

It was still dark in the room. He couldn't have slept long.

"They having some sort of limb trade-in program or something?" James asked.

David blinked repeatedly, trying to dislodge the sleep from his eyes. He could tell James was to his left, in the other bed.

As his vision cleared, he saw James there. His friend was more skeleton than man now, bones and sinew sporadically covered with decaying flesh. The gash down his face had grown wider, rotting away; his nose was gone completely. His eyes were wilted sacs, containing little hint of life. His teeth were infrequent, visible through holes in his tattered and deteriorating cheeks, past withered lips. His hair had been reduced to tufts, spotting his nearly bare and peeling, scabrous skull. His clothes were like rags now, dirty, torn, hanging limply on his withered and putrefying form. James seemed more a haunted house amusement than a true horror, and barely resembled the man he once was.

"I wouldn't talk if I were you," David murmured, trying to force a smile but failing; it simply wasn't in him anymore.

"Hey, I may not look like much," James said, sitting up on the bed, the bones in his jaw clacking together with each word. "But I'm not the one imagining a dead best friend, just so he has a buddy to talk to. You've got to get it together, Davey."

"I hate the name Davey," David said.

"I know."

James grinned. At least David thought it was a grin. The flaps of skin hanging from his skull pulled back around his mouth, and the spotted teeth locked together. The drooping bits of skin around his eyes narrowed. It was ghoulish.

"Not a good look for you, buddy," David said.

"I work with what I have," James replied. He rose, his legs moving awkwardly, barely under his control, and headed toward David's bed. He looked David up and down. "You've really become…rather pathetic, Davey."

"Fuck you."

"You're lost, buddy. And stubborn as shit. You're gonna be here forever."

David looked up at James' face. As horrible looking as James was, David still could see his childhood friend hidden there. He could smell the rotting flesh. "What do you want me to do?"

"Pay attention. Question what you see. Then take the journey."

"What does that even mean?" David said, aggravated; he let his head fall against the pillow.

"It's a riddle, and it's not even a very hard one," James said. "Does the dead guy have to spell it out for you?"

David sighed.

"Does any of this seem right to you, David?" James asked, leaning his bony frame against David's bed. "A hospital shut down by a snow storm, for…oh, how long have you been here now?"

How long have I been here now?

"You have no idea, right? Of course not. No phones. No communication. Crazy shit happening all the time. So, what is the answer? Are you crazy?"

"Maybe." David said.

James shook his head slightly. "Open your eyes. Do the work. Break the shell. Because pretty soon there won't be any shell left, friend. And then what will they burn?"

"I don't even understand what you're talking about," David said. "It's this goddamn place, James! It's driving me mad! What the hell is this place, anyway?!"

"*You* built this place. The moment you turned your back on it."

David shook his head. None of it made sense. "I've got to get out of here. I've got to get out."

"That's the last thing you want to do, David. If you get out of here…well, God help you." Slowly, James extended his bony hands and began to unfasten David's restraints. "Go and visit Virgil. Listen to him. He'll show you the way."

"This is all….This is madness," David said softly, closing his eyes. He could feel the pressure of the restraints being released.

"Yes," James whispered, pulling the blankets off of the bed, "perhaps you might call it that. But you have to look at it first, you have to face it, before you can call it anything at all."

David opened his eyes and looked up at James. James' face seemed sad, if that was even possible, given how little flesh was left to form expressions. James motioned at David's body.

"Look at yourself, and then call it madness if you want."

David looked up at the ceiling.

"Look at yourself, David," James said softly.

Gradually, David looked down. And he saw, for really the first time, his wounds, the absence of flesh, the new reality of his body. He shook his head and felt the emotions begin to come.

"Good," James said. "That's a start, buddy. Now, keep going."

202

David felt the tears start to bubble up, but then gritted his teeth and pushed them away, letting the anger rise up to take their place. He gripped the sheets with his hand and screamed at the top of his lungs.

It lasted seconds.

Then, for a moment, there was silence.

He turned to James, furiously. "What the fuck was that supposed to accomplish! Who do you even think you *are* to me anymore, you walking bag of meat!"

"David…" James sighed.

David seethed for a second, then released it, taking a deep, indignant breath. "I have…*nothing*…anymore."

"Go and see Virgil."

"And *how* exactly do you expect me to *do* that?" David snapped.

Without a word, James turned and wobbled clumsily into the hall and out of sight. When he returned, he was pushing a wheelchair. He placed it near David's bed and then moved to stand beside it.

"No," David whispered. "No fucking way."

"Got to do it, buddy," James said. "Got to do it."

"No."

"Okay, well then don't. And stay here forever," James turned and wobbled sluggishly back toward the other hospital bed. He climbed up onto the bed gracelessly, falling forward, letting his frail body drop onto the sheets. He seemed fatigued to David, like a battery-powered toy winding down. "I just want you…to let yourself be happy…for *once* in your goddamn adult life."

"I…I can't do it," David said.

"I think…that you can do anything," James said.

203

Then David watched as James' body began to collapse, tissues falling away from bones, bones withering into dust.

"I always have," James whispered with his last remaining strength, before his mouth and teeth began to crumble. "I love you, buddy."

Within moments, he was gone. Even his tattered clothes had broken down, dissolving into dust. And then the dust too disappeared into the air.

55

"How long do you think you can stay in that bed, David Daniel?"

Normally David was comforted by Virgil's deep tones, his casual, affable manner. Not today.

"I don't know," he said.

Virgil moved into the room, came close to the bed. "You need to move. We need to take the catheter out and you need to use the bathroom on your own. We need to work on the muscles you have. You're still a candidate for a prosthetic, boss, but not if you languish in bed."

David was silent. He stared at the ceiling.

"Whatever fear you have about the chair," Virgil continued, "is in your head. It's a tool. It's only a tool. And it's here to be of use to you."

"It's a curse," David whispered.

"No," Virgil replied, "it's just metal. And fabric. And spokes. It's no different than a bicycle, David."

You're doing it! It's all you.

"Why don't you let me help you?" Virgil asked.

David looked past him at the metal chair and shuddered. He took in its form, a formidable steel cage, just waiting for him. He let his eyes drift away, around the dim and dingy room, taking it all in, then he looked back at the chair once more, and finally to Virgil.

"I…I don't really have any choice, do I?" David asked, quietly.

Virgil nodded. "Sure you do. You can give up. You can lie here and die. And that doesn't seem like much of a choice at all."

David looked back at the chair again. He'd gone to great lengths to avoid anything to do with them his entire life, and here he was.

"Well," David sighed, "okay then." The air came up short in his lungs as he said the words, and he choked a bit.

Virgil smiled a consolatory smile and patted David's leg. "I'm going to get a nurse."

56

He could hear the water moving in his ears. The blood pulsed like a bullfrog behind his jaw.

Virgil had returned with the nurse, the one with the narrow bird-like face, and she had removed his catheter, changed his bed-pan, cleaned David, changed his bandages. Through the process, David had become a zombie, distant, disconnected with everything that was going on around him. Numb.

But now, as they carefully lifted him out of the bed, he realized the disconnection was failing him. He was here, more present than he ever wanted to be, and he felt as though he may explode.

The wheelchair loomed ahead of him, shining at him, beckoning to him, just as his mother's had, sitting at the foot of the stairs so many years before. But this time, it was claiming him. He had lost. He was going in to the chair, and there was nothing he could do anymore.

Everything seemed to slow.

David closed his eyes.

He could smell Virgil's cologne, just as he had before during their physical therapy time. It was a mellow smell, clean. But now it seemed acrid in his nostrils, stinging.

Slowly, they began to lower him down.

And then he felt the combination of metal and canvas beneath him.

They released him, allowing him to relax back into the chair, helping him to adjust. David felt it around him, surrounding him, cradling him.

He took a deep breath and held it. And then, he opened his eyes to his new reality.

57

The wheelchair could be powered with only one arm, Virgil had explained, and steered with only one foot. He'd walked with David down the hall a bit, and helped him to practice. David couldn't help but think that everyone was staring, secretly laughing at his disability, his incompetence in the machine.

"Trust me. It's better to use this than an electric model," Virgil had said. "You need to exercise the muscles you still have."

After a brief tour of the chair and jaunt down the hall, Virgil had accompanied David back to the room and showed him how best to use the bathroom facilities.

Moment by moment, David felt his soul eroding.

Now as he sat in the dark of Room 509, propped up in his bed, he truly wondered which thing was worse: a lifetime spent trapped in a metal cage or death.

The wind blew against his boarded windows, rousting him from his dark thoughts.

The storm seemed angry tonight.

How long have I been here? he wondered, glancing at the window. *When will this goddamn storm ever end? And where will I go when it does? Who will help me now?*

From his peripheral, David saw the lights in the hallway flicker and shut off briefly, replaced after a moment by the lights from the generator.

It was then that he turned and saw her standing in his doorway, silhouetted in dim light: the old woman with the kind face. She looked at him impassively and then over at the wheelchair. And then she turned to move off down the hallway.

"Wait," he said. His voice was much quieter than he'd anticipated.

And she was already gone.

Something inside told him to follow her, but he looked over at the chair and began to reconsider.

This is fucking ridiculous, he thought. *Are you going to let fear dictate your future?* Again, anger began to replace the fear he felt inside.

He set his jaw and then began to move his body to the edge of the bed. Gradually, he let his foot hang down and touch the floor. After he got his bearings, he rose slowly and balanced on one leg, learning that it was much harder to balance with only one arm. He leaned onto the chair, turned slightly, and let his body weight fall back.

As he landed in the cradle of the chair, he shuddered. It was something he didn't know how he'd ever get past. He wondered if someday, maybe, it wouldn't feel so terrifying, so utterly gruesome to him.

He began to turn the wheel backwards with his left hand, steering with his left foot, and was surprised that it was, even now, coming much more naturally than it had just hours before.

He pushed the chair forward, maneuvering to the doorway of the small hospital room, and he peeked out into the hall. The old woman was more than halfway down the dim corridor on the right, disappearing into an open doorway.

David steered the wheelchair into the hall and followed.

58

As he maneuvered down the long corridor, the tires of the wheelchair squeaking, longing for oil, he could hear the storm growing outside, shaking the building. It was getting hungrier.

He moved in the chair purposefully, both relieved and slightly horrified that guiding it came so naturally to him. His arm was easily fatigued, however. That would get easier with….

David sneered at his train of thought, snapped it off midstream. He didn't want to think about *time* spent in this chair. Or anymore *time* spent in this *place*. It had taken him apart, piece by piece, and he had no love for it at all. This *place*.

The building shook again, more violently, forceful enough to grab David's attention and cause him to wonder if there was a plan in place should something happen to the facility itself. Where does one evacuate to when they're already forsaken?

There's always the basement, he thought.

As he neared the room that the old woman had disappeared into, he slowed. There was music coming from within, voices. He pushed forward slightly, leaning in to see inside.

It was some sort of hospital gathering, it seemed. The room was multipurpose, arranged with folding tables and chairs. A table full of refreshments sat to one side. Nearly all of the staff was there, nurses and doctors alike. Many of them he recognized: Monica, Dr. Devar, the bird-faced nurse, the orderlies who had restrained him, and so on. So many familiar faces. Even people he'd passed once or twice in the hall.

What were they all doing here so late at night?

The music playing was older. At first David thought that it was Cab Calloway's "Minnie the Moocher." No, not that one, but similar: "The Ghost of Smokey Joe." His grandfather had listened to artists like Calloway compulsively right before he'd died, and so David recognized many songs from that era.

David pulled his wheelchair near the door, just out of sight, and watched them. It was definitely some sort of party. The attendees seemed happy, relaxed; they were all smiles. There was no hospital business going on tonight.

He couldn't see the old woman. She'd disappeared somewhere. And he didn't see Virgil either. But aside from them, it was a full cast of characters.

Some of the people hung by the refreshment table, drinking from small paper cups. Others swayed to the music, coming close to dancing, but not quite.

I guess they need to cut loose sometime too, he thought.

The wind shook the building urgently. David glanced behind him down the hall, worried that he'd be caught snooping, but the corridor was deserted.

Of course, he thought, *everyone's here.*

He watched as the people moved about, laughing and conversing, their eyes narrow and cheeks flush. The music seemed louder to him now. The first song ended and was replaced by a little known 60's tune, "Strychnine" by The Sonics. The segue was jarring.

Just then, two of the people moved aside, and David saw that Tammy was there in the room as well. He felt his body recoil involuntarily and then ease almost immediately. She was *here.* Not dead. He didn't know why he was surprised. He didn't know what was real at all anymore, and what was imagined.

He glanced down the hallway again, fearful of being discovered.

The party inside the room was growing louder now. Everyone seemed so happy, so free. Several of the nurses had begun to dance in earnest. One of them, a dark-haired woman he'd seen once or twice, was doing The Twist, raising her arms above her head, turning her body in a frenzy, smiling broadly. And as she lifted her hands up, fingers outstretched, something seemed to expand about her presence. David wasn't sure what it was at first. He leaned in quietly, and studied her. It seemed to have gotten darker around her head and arms, as if a shadow had passed over her body and stayed. But then he realized, the shadow hadn't passed over her. It was coming from within.

Long dark tendrils slithered out from inside of her, curling, unfolding like great black wings.

The others watched and smiled, nodding approvingly.

And then, in turn, each of them began to stretch out, extending fingers, uplifting their faces, allowing a dark core, at once unformed and still strangely tangible, to unfurl throughout the room. And as they did, their skin, like some unneeded corporeal binding, began to relax, loosen, and slide away. Until the room became full with a dark presence, growing and swirling like smoke, surging with an incontestable power.

David leaned in, hugging the doorway, hoping that the shadows of the hallway were enough to shield him from their gaze. He felt cold now. His skin, his tissues, felt dry and inert. He could feel himself growing unnaturally weary in spite of his panic. And yet, he stayed and watched, unable to break away. His breath was visible in the cold air.

The music throbbed. And one song led to another.

David could see what was left of Dr. Devar, now seemingly a mere husk of skin and matter, a discarded chrysalis sliding to the floor unneeded, trampled under the immensity of a dark thing that had emerged from within.

He tried to focus on the details of the creatures, to capture a mental picture of their appearance, but found it impossible to concentrate long enough. They were like great beasts made of shifting sands, ephemeral and evanescent. Like things made up of dreams, impossible to capture. He knew only that they were dark and that they were cold.

He felt that coldness leeching his energy, pulling at his insides, lapping at his very spirit.

David became panicked and pushed back in the chair quickly, forgetting in his haste to steer with his foot. The wheel turned the wrong direction, and scraped along the open door. Instantly, there was a flurry of motion from within the room, a swirling chaos. The dark things had been alerted to his presence.

David turned quickly in the chair and began to move down the hallway away from them, his arm powering the wheel of the chair as fast as he could. He glanced over his shoulder, hoping that he would see nothing at all, that he would've been beneath their notice.

But it was not so.

The dark things, built of murky smoke and ash, were in the hallway with him already, coming after him, chasing him down.

59

The hallways were dim, lit only from the emergency lights. The building shook and creaked and the windows rattled under the force of the storm. As David pushed the wheelchair down the hallway – not turning back for fear that the dark things would be on top of him, surrounding him, pulling him in to their murk – he found that he had become confused. The layout of the corridors seemed to have changed. Where was his little room? The intersecting hallway? Where was he?

He could feel the coldness of them on the back of his neck and down his arm.

David turned the chair to the right quickly and headed down another hallway, hoping to evade their icy tendrils, confuse their incorporeal forms. He turned again, left this time. His arm was on fire from the strain, but he continued to turn the wheel. His breathing was labored.

So tired.

Another right. He'd never been here. He didn't even recognize this place. His memory drifted back – how far he didn't even know – to the night he'd first hazarded out on his crutches, to the confused YOU ARE HERE sign, mixed up, jumbled, and incomprehensible. He felt very much like he was navigating *those* hallways now.

The building shook violently. It seemed like any minute the structure would be torn apart, ripped and ravaged under the claws of the storm. As if the hallway would collapse and he would be sent flying out into the snow, cold and alone, back to where this all began.

He put his head down and pushed harder. He thought he could see the dark coils from his peripheral vision, reaching out toward him, around him, ready to envelop the entirety of his being.

He turned down another hallway on the right, cutting close to the corner. And there he had to brake and turn quickly to avoid knocking Virgil down.

"Hey!" Virgil bellowed.

David felt the wheelchair list to the side under the momentum, teeter on the verge of tumbling over, and then skid into the wall and stop.

"Whoa! Where are you goin', boss?"

David's heart was racing. He turned feverishly and watched the corner, waiting for the things to come, waiting for them to glide around the corner on cloudy black wings like shadowy ghosts and flow over him en masse, a billowy biting darkness.

But they did not come.

"Where are you goin' in such a damn hurry?" Virgil asked again, placing a large hand on David's shoulder. "You okay? You look pale."

"They're after me," David said.

Virgil scowled. "Who? Who's after you, boss?"

David decided to tell Virgil the truth, no matter how absurd it sounded. He had nothing to lose. Hiding all of the insanity he'd experienced since arriving in this place had served no good purpose. How much worse could the truth be?

"The…staff. They turned…into creatures, dark creatures, like smoke. Cold and black. I saw them. And they chased me." David was short of breath but his voice was even. He looked Virgil in the eye as he said the words.

Virgil frowned, shaking his head slightly.

"It's true," David said. "I saw them slip off their skin like clothes. They're…they're demons."

"You didn't see demons," Virgil said quietly. "David, there aren't demons here."

David sniggered, turning his head away. "Then what did I see, Virgil? What was…what was just chasing me?"

Virgil squatted down near the wheelchair, and put a hand on it. He took a moment before speaking. "Maybe you need to go back and look, David. To really look. And see. There's no one in this hospital trying to hurt you. I promise. Only those who are trying to help."

"Does this look HELPFUL?!" David shouted, lifting his limbless shoulder toward Virgil. "Do I look HELPED to you?!" His voice echoed in the hall.

Virgil's expression was calm, always calm. But he didn't smile now. He regarded David steadily, seriously. "David, all of the things you *think* you're seeing, they're all just…your perceptions…of things." He stopped. It was obvious he was choosing his words carefully. "I can tell you that there are no… *demons*…here. Only others like you, and we're trying to *help* you. But *you* have to believe that. *You* have to allow yourself to be helped. And sometimes…well, sometimes, that's a painful thing."

David looked at Virgil and drew his lips up over his teeth in a sneer. "What do you…you don't know!" David shook his head, smiling frantically. "You don't know what *I've* seen! Who the *fuck* are you?"

The remark seemed to sadden Virgil and he looked away. "Just a friend, David. Just someone, like the rest, who is trying to help."

"Well you've done a *shit job,*" David said snidely.

He looked at Virgil with contempt.

"Don't do this," Virgil whispered. "You're gonna be all alone, David. Don't do this."

David sneered at him, chuckling slightly. He stared into the big man's dark eyes and realized, with certainty, that he had been wrong to let him in, wrong to trust him. Virgil was just another one of *them.*

Just then, David saw something move under the skin on Virgil's cheek. And there was something else: a darkness had invaded Virgil's eyes, spreading out over the whites with spider-like fingers, engulfing his eyeballs until there was nothing there but the deepest black.

David moved away from him quickly, pushing the wheelchair in reverse, backing and turning out into the hallway. As he moved away, he could hear Virgil's transformation continue behind him, a sloughing off of tissue, a fluttering of smoky wings.

He pushed the wheelchair down the corridor once more, and he could see the rest of them ahead, a weighty darkness gathered at the end of the hallway, advancing toward him. David turned the wheelchair to the left, and moved down another hallway, just in front of the swirling dark. He could hear them fluttering behind him, could feel the warmth leeching away, the oxygen drawing thin. He could see his breath again.

But the hallway was a dead end.

Ahead of him was the elevator, doors open; it seemed to wait for him. There were no other hallways, no other open doors. No escape. He felt his wheelchair pulling away from the cold, from the darkness, yet there was nowhere else to go.

Unless you count the basement, which I do not.

Nowhere but down.

He rolled into the elevator fast, sliding to an abrupt stop against the back wall. He turned and mashed his palm on the CLOSE button.

He looked behind him into the corridor and watched as the great darkness grew closer. And closer still. As it floated and poured toward him, engulfing the hallway, an incomprehensible mass of swirling shadow. The emergency lighting dimmed and then faded into nothingness, extinguished by its presence.

Ten and then fifteen feet at a time, it came, rolling toward him like a giant wave of night, a churning, chirring wall of ebony.

"Come on," David whispered urgently, pressing the letter B repeatedly. "Come on."

And just as the darkness was upon him, just as it moved to overtake him, the elevator doors slid shut and the elevator began to descend.

To the basement.

60

The elevator descended slowly, mechanisms grinding and whirring in the shaft above. David allowed himself to breathe, allowed his body to un-tense. His arm throbbed and ached, stiff from overuse.

He realized, despondently, that he'd gone from one dead end to another. There was no way that the basement would offer him escape, only new obstacles. And he didn't imagine that the dark things would relent now, not now that he'd seen them, not now that he knew. They wouldn't stop until they'd taken him in, consumed him.

As the elevator continued its descent, creeping into the basement, David realized that there was no one left who could help him, no one he could turn to. No one he could trust. Virgil had been the last of them.

He was alone.

The elevator stopped with a jerk. There was a momentary pause as the compartment settled, and then the doors began to slide open.

It opened onto a large room, dim and cold and slightly dank. The walls and floors, even the cabinet and tables, were all the same monochromatic palette: grays and blues and dark blues and chromes.

The floor was covered in small dusty blue tile. At the far side of the room was row upon row of metal compartments, stacked three high, each several feet wide by several feet tall. And in the middle of the room stood a table, low profiled and sterile looking, cold. It was steel with polished metal legs. On the table lay a body, dressed only in a hospital gown. It was pale. A tag hung from its toe.

This was the morgue. David had expected no less, but still, it was unnerving to him to be there.

He moved out of the elevator and into the room, pushing the chair forward cautiously. There were no windows, and no other doors that he could see. It was, indeed, another dead end, in more ways than one.

David allowed the doors to the elevator to close behind him, and then cursed himself. He moved to the call button, and pushed it frantically, hoping to recall the cab before it departed, but it was too late. He could hear it moving up. It would return to the main floor within seconds, and then anyone – *anything* – could follow him down.

He shook his head, realizing that he wouldn't be able to run much longer. He pushed the wheelchair into the room toward the body on the table and examined the surroundings, hoping to find a closet or storage room to hide within. As he got closer to the body, he realized that he recognized it. It was Curtis, the old man he'd spoken to in the recreation room. A pang of regret shot through David. He liked the old man and hadn't wanted him to be the one who had passed.

The old man's face was gaunt and his mouth hung agape. His eyes stared at the ceiling. It was disconcerting to see them open and fixed in such a way, but David remembered hearing that the eyes would open again involuntarily after death. He remembered a friend in elementary school talk about morticians having to sew the eyes of the dead shut. He didn't know if that was true, but he had wondered about it when his mother died. Had her eyes been sewn shut too, to see no more?

David found himself staring at Curtis, a husk of what he'd been merely – *days?* – before, staring at his lifeless eyes. And then, ever so slowly, the eyes began to move. They rolled to the side and looked at David. He jumped back slightly and felt a chill on his neck.

And then, almost unbearably, Curtis winked.

David turned his head away and closed his eyes. *No more,* he thought. *Too much.* He spun the chair in the opposite direction and moved on without looking back at Curtis, determined to ignore what had happened and find a storage room.

And then he heard something new: a knocking sound.

David turned his head and listened.

Knock, knock, knock.

It was firm, but muffled, almost metallic. David glanced back over his shoulder, just to make sure Curtis' body was still there. It was.

Knock, knock, knock.

He looked back at the elevator. Was it the mechanism turning? Was the cab headed back down already?

Knock, knock, knock.

No. It was coming from the far side of the room, the metallic compartments. The refrigerators. It was coming from within.

Knock, knock...knock.

David felt another chill, felt the gooseflesh on his arm. Was someone *trapped* inside one of the refrigerators?

He pushed the wheelchair a bit closer and listened intently.

Knock...knock...knock.

It was coming from one near the ground, to his right. He moved closer still, and leaned in.

Knock...knock...knock.

A voice inside of him warned him not to open it. To move away, to find a hiding place and let it be. But he had to know. He couldn't let it pass. He placed his trembling hand on the handle near the door.

Knock. Knock....

And then he pulled.

The door opened and the tray moved out slightly, automatically. On it was a body bag, zipped up. And something was moving underneath.

Move away, David thought. *There's no way whatever this is could've been knocking. Its arms are restrained.*

But as if on autopilot, David's hand reached out and gripped the zipper. And then he began to pull it back. He watched as a face was revealed, a man with a bloody slit for a mouth, his eyes wide in terror, his skin pale and rubbery.

The man turned his head slightly and looked into David's eyes. The cut where his mouth should be was open wide, sucking air, and then he whispered. "The dead do not know…anything," he hissed. The flesh on the top and bottom of his jagged mouth rubbed together like raw meat. "Nor have they any longer a reward, for their memory is…forgotten."

David pushed back, and as he did, he saw the man's face begin to change. It was subtle, almost a trick of the light, but it happened. He saw it. The face transformed itself into an image of David, a dark reflection with a ragged wound for a mouth.

"The living know they will die," it spoke, "but the dead… do not know anything."

It began to move, to writhe in its body bag.

David pushed back further and turned, but as he did, he could hear the elevator descending again.

He was too late.

He turned to face it as the elevator doors began to open.

61

As the elevator doors slid open, the hospital shook and rocked ferociously, and David felt the wheelchair shudder underneath him, the wheels sliding of their own volition.

He watched the doors open and steeled himself, preparing for the worst.

But no sentient darkness emerged. Just people: a blonde man, an older balding man, and a younger woman. The blonde man, David recognized; he'd been in the recreation room that day, he'd been watching the news.

The blonde man reached out and held the elevator doors, but none of them moved into the basement. "Are you coming?" he barked. "This place is fallin' apart!"

David was confused, but he nodded and moved quickly toward them. He glanced back at the refrigerator door. He wasn't sure what he'd see, but he was surprised to see it closed again; he didn't know why anything shocked him anymore, but it did.

As he rolled into the elevator, the building rocked again viciously. His wheelchair rolled diagonally and he hit the brake, stopping just short of the wall; the young woman jumped aside. The overhead lights in the basement were swaying.

"Is this safe?" the balding man asked, indicating the elevator.

"We'll make it up one floor," replied the blonde man.

The young woman was visibly flustered. "It's all coming undone," she murmured.

David had gone from living in his own personal horror movie to a surreal disaster film in mere seconds. He wondered where they could possibly go if they needed to evacuate the hospital, especially with him in a wheelchair. Weren't they leaving the safest place they could possibly be?

He wondered too about the dark things, where they had retreated to, if anyone else had seen them.

As the elevator ascended, the building shook again around them. The balding man was thrown off balance and lurched into the blonde man. The lights above them flickered and then went out, leaving the small cab in darkness. The elevator lurched and then stopped.

"Alright, alright, just *calm down!*" the blonde man barked in the darkness. "The generator *will* come back online."

They became still and waited.

The young woman was whimpering slightly, or perhaps it was the balding man; David wasn't sure. It was as dark as he could recall, as dark as the supply closet had been, at least. And David remembered what had happened in there – *or had it?* Again, he found himself peering into darkness, willing his eyes to adjust.

It was still. They could hear the sounds from above: the violent whipping winds, the shattering of metal and glass, the sound of people screaming, fleeing.

For an instant, he wondered if he was alone there in the dark, lost in it. If maybe the dark things had found him after all, devoured him when he wasn't looking. But then the young woman whispered, "How do you know the generator will come back on?"

The blonde man didn't answer. And the stillness continued.

David wondered about the sounds upstairs. Was it truly the storm doing all of this damage, or was it the darkness itself, the large fluttering ashen wings of the dark things as they tore through the hospital, engulfing everything in their path.

And then, he felt a familiar touch on his arm. And in the darkness, he heard her, near him, closer than he expected anything to be. The immediacy made him jump back in his chair.

"Daaaaaaviiiiid."

He felt his breath catch, his heart race.

He couldn't dare imagine that this was happening. He couldn't, he *wouldn't* allow himself to be trapped there in the darkness with…her. With *it*.

"Daaaaaviiiiiiid," it whispered.

"Go away!" David yelled.

"Looooook at meeeeee," the voice came, right by his ear. He could feel hot breath on his skin.

"GO AWAY!"

Suddenly, the lights returned.

It was just the four of them. And the others were looking in his direction, regarding him apprehensively. The blonde man leaned over and pushed the M button, and the elevator began to rise again.

"Where do you want we should go, pal?" he said.

David said nothing in return, just looked away.

Insanity, if that's what this was, was beginning to take its toll on him. He couldn't handle any more.

Soon, the elevator arrived at the main floor, and the doors opened in front of them. The hospital was crumbling, falling to pieces before their eyes.

The white of the snow was invading through cracks in the building's architecture, surging in through collapsing walls, whipping through the dimly lit air, coating the now slick floors.

The patients were panicked, running, scattered.

The staff, however, was nowhere to be seen.

62

The others moved out of the elevator around him and dispersed. The blonde man looked him up and down. "You gonna be okay?"

No, of course not, you idiot.

David nodded.

The blonde man disappeared down the hall.

Why had they come to the basement in the first place? Where were they intending to go? Shouldn't they all stay underground?

David reached out and held the doors of the elevator, and considered going back down to the basement by himself. But then he remembered the man in the refrigerator and Curtis winking at him. He thought of being stuck in the dark of the elevator again, this time all on his own. No, he couldn't do it. He couldn't. He'd have to face the chaos of the hospital, come what may.

He rolled out into the hallway. It was cold, bitter cold. In only a hospital gown, it wouldn't take long for him to be affected by the harsh elements. He knew that much. And maybe that was okay.

It was hard to move on the slick tile floors. He felt the wheels drifting.

Impossible. This is…impossible.

David shook his head, and stopped, looking up and down the corridor. From a distance, he could still hear screaming and commotion, but there wasn't much activity at all around him. The building rocked again, shook under another assault. The wind tore at the walls, peeling them further and further back, allowing the outside in.

David felt still and quiet. Calm almost.

He watched the snow pour through an opening in the wall of the hospital with fascination, mesmerized. He moved his wheelchair closer to the opening and locked the wheels down.

He felt the wind whip at his face and hair. He peered out into the cold, the blinding white of the storm, and realized that he felt somewhat content there. Relaxed, even.

Freezing, if he recalled, was a comfortable way to die.

Even then, he was losing feeling in his remaining fingers and toes.

Then, he could see something else there in the ice, obscured by the ceaseless flurries. He stared hard, squinting against the snow. And then realized that what he was seeing was an overturned car. No, a Jeep.

There had been an accident.

He thought about turning, alerting someone. But whom?

As he looked, the snow seemed to part under his gaze, and the scene became familiar. There were two men lying in the snow on their bellies. The Jeep had overturned and it was resting on one of them, crushing his right side. The tire of the Jeep turned slowly in the air under its own momentum. The other man was staring sightlessly, his cheek down on the snow, his eyes locked open.

It was *them,* he realized, he and James. It was *their* accident. And it looked so much worse now than he'd imagined. He wondered how he'd ever survived it. How he'd ever been found.

It was a figment of his imagination, he knew. A byproduct of slowly freezing to death in a blizzard. But still, it was fascinating to him and he couldn't look away. And as he sat there at the edge of an improvised doorway, an uneven window unto a vicious and violent world, David realized that it was all okay. He was actually *happy* to be coming full circle. It all felt right.

His body was shuddering, but he couldn't feel the cold anymore. Or his lips, his fingers, his face. The wind tore at his gown, at his hair.

David closed his eyes and smiled.

63

When he opened his eyes again, it was daytime. And it was quiet in Room 509. The sounds of the storm had gone away. He could only hear a television droning on down the hall.

"Good morning," Dr. Devar said as she entered the room. She was smiling.

David jumped upon seeing her, a knee-jerk response.

"Are you feeling any better?" she asked.

His eyes moved around the room: the walls were the same dreary yellow he remembered, showing no signs of storm damage. His skin, which had gone numb under the cold, was smooth and pliable.

"No," he said, "I don't feel very well at all."

She nodded. "I expected as much. You've been fighting a fairly strong infection since the amputation of your arm. Your fever got very high last night. Do you recall?"

No, he had no memory of that at all. Just of her turning into a great dark thing.

She nodded again. "That's okay. Just get some rest." She patted his arm and moved to his chart.

"But…how…the storm…" he mumbled.

She smiled at him. "The storm is over. They cleared the roads this morning. You're going to be leaving us…provided your fever stays down."

"What? When did…but…where am I going?" he asked, a desperation creeping into his voice.

Just then, Monica entered followed by a tall, dark-haired man with a large, gleaming white smile and narrow eyes. His hair was slicked back, and he was wearing a suit that David recognized as expensive; it was a Zegna if he wasn't mistaken.

"David," Monica said, "this is Peter Routh, he works for your company. He's here to help you. "

Yes, David recognized him now. *Routh.* They hadn't had much interaction, but Peter seemed like an okay, if overly zealous, guy. David wondered why *he* was here.

"Hey there, sport," Routh said, resting on the edge of David's bed. Routh was being careful not to let his eyes wander over to David's amputations, and that resulted in prolonged, insincere eye contact.

"I'll be down the hallway finishing up the discharge paperwork," Monica said. She smiled awkwardly at David, a final tiny gesture before she disappeared into the hallway.

"You are *quite lucky* to be alive, my friend," Routh said, his large white teeth displayed.

"Yeah, that's what everyone keeps saying," David replied.

Routh laughed heartily as if David had just said the funniest thing he'd ever heard. It made David want to punch him in the throat.

"Boy, I bet," Routh smirked.

"Why you?" David asked.

Routh stopped chuckling and raised his eyebrows. "Come again?"

"Why you? Why are you here? Why did they send...*you?*"

Routh's forehead creased and he puzzled the question. "Well, I don't know. I mean, who else would you expect?"

David thought about it. Everyone above him in the company was far too busy for a job like this. And since he didn't really associate much with those below him, Routh being chosen actually made a great deal of sense. He was an errand boy. And David was an errand. He was just lucky, he supposed, that they sent anyone at all.

"Whatever. Fuck it. I'm just glad I'm going home," David said.

"Well, we're not going *home*." Routh chuckled again, a bit nervously. "The…uh…*doctors* here think you require a bit more…*supervision,* and we at the company tend to agree with them. So we're going to take you somewhere a bit…special." He winked at David and patted his leg.

David wanted to set his Routh's hair on fire.

"Okay then?" Routh said. It was a rhetorical question. It did nothing but fill the silence.

David looked from him to Dr. Devar, and she nodded.

And as he looked at her, he could see the movement under her skin, the subtle rolling of a hidden dark form.

PART VIII: THE BLACK

64

It had been nearly five years since David's time at Elysian Falls General Hospital. Nearly five years since the accident. Since the dark things had first come. Since they'd begun to visit him in earnest; the beginning of what would be a slow downward spiral into madness.

David sat in his wheelchair against the drawn shades in the corner of the common room of Mount Hood Sanatorium. He was a man older than his years, grizzled, withered, tired. His hair and beard were prematurely gray.

He sat there and watched, and he waited, alone. Now that he knew, his days were lived in a near constant state of vigilance, his nights spent with one eye open, drifting in and out of a shallow and tenuous sleep.

He watched and waited.

For signs of them.

They had often left him alone for long periods of time, drawing him into a false sense of security. Once, as long as six months had gone by with no contact. He'd almost started to believe that the doctors had been right all along, that it had all been a figment of his imagination. And he'd begun to feel like he might be able to leave this place one day. David told his doctor at the time – an older man, dull in countenance, an academic by the name of Dr. Porter – about his progress, half expecting them to talk about moving toward a release date, toward finally getting David back into the real world where he belonged. Instead, he'd seen the doctor's mask slip away slightly, the skin on his face ripple, a brief window into the darkness behind, and he'd known then, he'd become absolutely certain, that Porter was one of them too.

Of course, the doctor had realized that he'd slipped. David had seen the raised eyebrow, the slightly guilt-ridden look. Porter had reached up and removed his glasses anxiously, rubbing his eyes, no doubt to hide the little adjustments he was making to the skin on his face, smoothing the mask so that it was perfect once again.

David realized then that he'd become too lax, been lulled in. Oh, they'd been patient, waiting for him to relax. Waiting for the right time.

It wasn't long after that that the other patient had tried to sneak into David's room in the middle of the night and kill him. Bruno Costa was a large man, half Cuban, half Italian, and not all right in the head. Bruno – once the owner of a chain of dry cleaners, back before he'd lost all his marbles – had come clumsily, oafishly, in the night, wandering into David's room, a butter knife in hand, whistling "How Much is That Doggie in the Window." But David had been ready for him. He'd waited behind the door of his room in his wheelchair, gripping a crutch in his left hand like a baseball bat.

And he'd beaten Bruno so badly with it that the man had died from his injuries. Well, not Bruno, not exactly. The dark thing that wore Bruno's face. *That* had died. David didn't feel bad about Bruno. Bruno, he assumed had died long before.

He'd been so close to leaving that time, he thought. So close. But they'd seen to it that he wasn't going anywhere. Not for a very long time. Maybe not forever.

A year later, the doctors informed him, quite unemotionally, that he had diabetes. And less than a year after that, they'd forcibly taken his left foot from him. They'd come under cover of night and drugged him, taken him into an operating room against his will, and they'd removed yet another piece of him.

David wasn't surprised they'd done it. He wasn't surprised at anything they did to him anymore. He was simply waiting for it to all be over. And so, he watched, waiting for them to reappear, determined to take as many of them to hell along with him.

Now, he sat in the corner of the room watching the others, each in various states of mental breakdown, and he wondered which one of them might be next to come at him.

All he really wanted was peace.

65

The nurse leaned in to his room where he sat quietly. She was one of the newer ones, middle-aged, redheaded, flat-faced, slightly overweight. He wondered at one point in time if the newer ones were to be trusted less or more than the others, but decided eventually that they were all equally worthy of his mistrust and suspicion.

"David, you have a visitor," she said.

He bristled a bit. He didn't know who it could be. There was no one left in his life that even remembered he was here, as far as he could tell. At one point, not long after he'd arrived, Dana had attempted to come. He'd been sitting by his window in his wheelchair, silently watching the outside world as he often did, when he glimpsed her climbing out of her car. At first, he couldn't believe it was really her, limping along on a cane as she did, but the way she flipped her hair, her unmistakable profile, the color of her lipstick, her smile; it hadn't taken much for him to be convinced. But as she'd come around the passenger side, another man had gotten out; he was tall, dark haired, pleasant looking. He'd gripped her shoulders and they'd talked seriously a moment; David figured he could guess the man's words: *I'll be right here if you need me.* And then the man had kissed her, and they'd embraced.

David had declined to see her.

And no one else had ever come.

Not until today.

"Who is it?" he asked, quietly.

66

David hovered close to the door of his room and listened into the hall. Two voices, both female. He wondered if the nurse realized he could hear them speaking about him when they got this close. Or perhaps she imagined that the patients simply disappeared once the doors to their tiny rooms were closed, burdens stowed away neatly, like so much silverware in a drawer.

"He still imagines things. Creatures. Demons out to get him. He hasn't had a bad outburst in a while, but he's been on restricted privileges since the incident with the Costa man. He's always being monitored."

As he suspected.

It was the same flat-faced nurse, from the sound of her nasally drawl.

"And his illness?" the other voice asked. It was an older voice, warm, congenial.

"His diabetes is very bad. His diet is restricted, but he sneaks food. He doesn't exercise. He's in generally bad health. He seems to have…given up." And then she added, "You should know, he's not a very pleasant human being now, if he ever was."

There was a pause, and then: "I'll see him now, if that's all right."

David rolled back from the door and positioned himself near the window. He was unshaven and ungroomed, as had become customary for him, and his beard was rough and chaotic looking. He regretted that just a bit, now that he was going to have a visitor. He pulled a blanket over his lap, and made sure it covered his legs, or what was left of them.

The door opened.

He didn't recognize the woman who entered. She was older, gray-haired, and kind-faced. She was wearing a black dress with gold piping, and a small black hat, slightly askew. She appeared as if she'd stepped out of a 1960s movie, but the look suited her. He could tell her hair was longer, and pinned up elegantly, although tiny strands had gone astray. Her face was cragged but still soft looking, moisturized. She gripped a tiny black purse in front of her with both hands, each covered in a dainty black glove. She seemed familiar, but he couldn't recall from where.

"Hello, David," she said.

"Do I know you?" he asked brusquely.

She smiled a somewhat pained smile and shook her head. He scrutinized her. It would be just like *them* to send a representative in such a non-threatening form. He would be cautious.

She moved into the room, pulled a chair away from the wall, and sat. "Although, you may *remember* me. I was at Elysian Falls too, back when you had your accident."

His eyes narrowed, searching his recollection for her. And then he remembered. But wait, it wasn't possible. The person he was thinking of had seemed old to him then, a kindly woman smiling at him as he came out of surgery, a presence in the halls. It was all muddled now, the time spent in that hospital, faded, but he remembered her being old then. And she seemed no older to him now.

She could see him puzzling.

"I've aged well," she said.

He nodded. "Okay. So? What do you want?"

"I wanted to check on you. You were so…*confused* then. Angry. I was hoping you'd gotten yourself together…figured it all out."

238

He inhaled deeply, chuckling. "And what do you think?"

She shook her head.

"You're dying, David. It won't be long. You know that, right? That you're dying?"

It was bracing to hear the words spoken so nakedly, directly to his face and not behind his back. *Dying.*

"About fucking time," he said.

"I don't believe you mean that."

"Good for you. So, is that it?" he asked curtly. A part of him liked having a visitor, speaking to another human who was neither staff nor fellow patient. But another, much larger part, a part obsessed with self- preservation, found it altogether too taxing.

"I'd like to tell you a story."

"I'd rather...you didn't."

The woman looked at him, her eyes steady and nonjudgmental. He bristled under her expression, found himself looking away.

"It's about a woman. A woman who was blessed with a beautiful life. A loving, though sometimes thick-headed husband, and a wonderful little boy she loved with all of her self."

David opened his mouth, intending to tell the woman to leave, but he stopped. The words didn't come. He felt anxious suddenly, felt his heart beating in his chest.

"She might've been the happiest woman who had ever walked the face of the earth."

The woman placed the purse in her lap and removed the black gloves slowly, placing each one inside her bag.

"One day, she was walking home from the store, carrying groceries for the family. She had bought Rocky Road ice cream, which was her son's favorite. And she was eager to give it to him because he always got so excited about even the tiniest little present.

"When she got to the corner, down the street from their little house, she saw a car coming toward her, somewhat... unsteady. It all happened fast. She could see the woman behind the wheel. The woman was young, possibly too young to drive, and scared. The car was out of her control."

David felt himself begin to sweat. "Who are you?" he asked, but the answer wasn't as important to him as he thought it should be. He wanted to hear what she was going to say. The anger he was so used to cloaking his words and actions with felt out of place now, unsuitable.

She continued: "The woman could see panic on the young girl's face. She had only moments to act. It all happened... in the blink of an eye. To jump left...or right? She dove to the side at the last possible moment, and the car, which was almost certainly destined to hit her, lurched over the curb, and careened away down the street."

"What?"

"She was shaken, the woman. But after a while, she didn't even think of it again. Her little boy was so pleased to see the ice cream, and never even knew how close his mother had come to getting hit. Her husband hugged her, and they all sat down to dinner, just like they normally did. And not a word was spoken about the car.

"Well, the years passed and the little boy grew into a handsome young man. He was top of his class, did well at sports, and was kind to everyone he met. His mother and he were very close. His father took him fishing every month, and the two talked. The young man even convinced his father to quit smoking, but that didn't stop him from developing a debilitating disease, one that eventually took his life.

"By the time that happened, the young man had gotten home from college, where he'd been studying to be a doctor. He'd met a lovely young woman at school and they'd made plans to be married. And when his father died, the young man stood next to his mother, and he gave the eulogy."

David felt tears come into his eyes. He tried to remember the last time he'd felt them there. His hand was shaking.

"The young man had suddenly become a patriarch, and had made plans to start a family of his own. A baby boy was born, and several years later, a baby girl. He named the boy after his father. And his mother loved her grandchildren. She spoiled them. She adored her daughter-in-law, and watched with pride as the son she'd raised nurtured a family of his own, watched as he went to work as a doctor and saved lives. And she was *so* proud of him."

"Who are you?" David whispered, tears streaming down his cheeks. "Why are you doing this?"

"You're fading, David. You're near the end of yet *another* cycle. And I don't want you to have to do this all over again. Not another time. I want you…to be at peace."

David felt sick, felt his body shaking. "Why…are you telling me this?"

"Because that's not what happened. Because the woman jumped left when she should have jumped right. Because the Rocky Road melted in the sun next to her broken body. But she still wanted all of the rest for her son. She never wanted anything less. She never wanted him to be so…*angry.*"

"I don't…I can't…"

"Yes, you can, sweetheart. Yes, you can."

"I can't…"

"Just let go, David. Just let go…I've got you."

He felt the waves of sadness wash over him, felt his body begin to convulse as his hand went over his face, guarding tears that had waited too long to come. He ached as spasms of sadness coursed through his tired form.

And his memory was flooded with so many events from his life. But they all seemed different now. For a moment, he was able to see himself as he was, stubbornly refusing to care, turning his back on those he loved at his own injury. Images from the hospital flowed through his mind, him standing with a kitchen knife, tearing into his own arm. Broken down in a supply closet, overcome with memories of a lost love, unable to follow through on a senseless act. A roomful of new friends staging an intervention. Friends, not demons, not great dark things hunting him down.

His shoulders heaved under his sobs.

"I'm sorry," he choked. "Oh God, I'm so sorry."

"It's okay, David. Just let go," the old woman repeated. "Just let go. I've got you."

67

David found himself drifting languidly down a long hallway lit from above by fluorescent lights, which made yellow walls appear sickly. In the background, he could hear the squeaking of small wheels on tile. The beeping of machines. "Moonlight Sonata."

His body ached. His hand was shaking. Had he passed out?

At the end of the hallway was a dark room. His body floated along toward it.

Was someone laughing? Were those footsteps? So much ambient noise here now, creeping in. He tried to hum along to "Moonlight Sonata," but it came out as nothing more than a groan.

"Just a minute, David, we're almost there."

His body glided down the hallway, propped upright in the hand of the wheelchair, propelled by an unseen force. David tilted his head upward sluggishly and saw that it was the old woman who was pushing him forward. She looked down at him, smiling compassionately, guiding the wheelchair on, down the hallway, toward the darkness.

David closed his eyes again.

68

As they came down the mountain pass, David cranked the heater on the Jeep; it was almost too warm now. Better than outside, he figured. They were more than halfway down the mountain now and the snow was still deep on the sides of the road, with new snow falling. His windshield wipers went on and off, intermittently.

"Yeah, but…I can't see them renewing it for another season," James said, taking a bite off his pre-packaged pepperoni stick. "It's *cool,* but there's no audience. No one gets it."

"Well, I've never seen it."

"And that's part of the problem," James said enthusiastically, small bits of meat flying out of his mouth. "There's no promotion at all. What do they expect?"

"Well, I just think it's cool you got to work on a show at all," David replied. "Besides, now you've got a credit."

"An *assistant* credit. On a show no one's heard of!"

"Still a credit."

James laughed. "I should leave it to you to look for the 'glass is half full' angle."

David smiled. *Maybe so.*

"Oh hey, did Dana let you know about dinner?" James asked.

David nodded. The roads were getting slick. He'd have to watch that. "She said she's good to go. She found a sitter."

"Awesome. This is going to be fun. We never get to hang out, all four of us, anymore."

It *had* been hard since the baby had come.

James turned David's iPod up to catch the end of The Smiths' "How Soon is Now," which gave way to The White Stripes' "You're Pretty Good Looking."

"I can't believe you're still listening to this band. I'm surprised anyone is!" James derided.

"What? The hell you say!"

"They're overrated," James said. "They're a garage band that got lucky. Right place, right time."

"Have you seen them live?" David asked.

"Right. Like *that's* going to happen!"

"C'mon man, they're raw," David protested. "They have passion."

James scoffed, and tore into another package of pepperoni.

"Life is messy sometimes," David continued. "It's not all fine-combed, auto-tuned, processed. They're messy, raw, passionate. They're what rock-and-roll is all about!"

"Whatever you say, brother," James smiled. "Whatever you say."

David reached for his coffee mug in the center console, and as he did, he felt the tires slip on a patch of black ice. The steering wheel wobbled. And he jerked, instinctively, trying to compensate, but he felt the car list, and begin to spin.

The car rocked, trembled. He could see the guard rail in front of them. His foot hit the break to no effect.

The tires squealed in the snow.

At least he thought that's what the noise was.

It was either that or the shriek of the metal guardrail. The wail of the trees as they bent sideways, scraping down the sides of the Jeep.

Maybe it wasn't the tires at all.

He wondered if they were even touching the ground anymore. He wondered why he had the time to be wondering anything. It all seemed to be happening in slow motion, as if it were happening to someone else. As if it weren't even real.

His hands on the steering wheel felt numb.

He felt the vehicle list to the side and became vaguely aware of the seatbelt cutting into his neck. His eyes drifted languidly to the rearview mirror, and he caught a fleeting glimpse of his own unshaven face, accepting, his dark hair standing straight up, defying gravity.

The scenery in front of the Jeep shifted, an impressionist painting of pine and snow. The windshield cracked. And he suddenly became aware of James screaming.

He heard the sound of metal bending. Felt the compartment of the Jeep shifting around them. Tasted blood in his mouth.

Dana, he thought. *I'm so sorry.*

69

A moment of bright white – the sun reflecting off the snow, perhaps, intruding on the compartment of the Jeep – and then darkness.

He could hear the sound of the vehicle settling, rocking in place, the sound of air escaping from…somewhere.

He found the darkness agreeable, comforting, like a warm blanket.

Open your eyes, David.

It was his father's voice.

Open your eyes, David. We're Graces.

His eyelids fluttered and a blade of vivid white pierced the veil. There was blood in his eyes. Strange. He didn't feel injured at all. Just comfortable. He blinked as if he could dismiss the liquid like the remnants of a deep sleep.

He became aware, quite suddenly, that it was cold. His stomach, his arms, freezing. He was lying in the snow, on the ice. His heavy jacket hadn't been needed in the warmth of the Jeep, not with its hardcover top latched down and the heater going full blast. David was lying in the snow in his shirtsleeves.

He felt a twinge move through him. And he closed his eyes again.

It was safe in the darkness.

His brain seemed to loosen inside his skull, and float away. He imagined it disintegrating, piece by piece, atom by atom, moving out across the outer darkness, spreading itself so thin that it was no longer visible anymore. Still there, but improved, a part of something larger. He imagined it as a beautiful sandcastle, once meticulously crafted by tiny hands, now slowly eroding away, simply becoming part of the beach once more.

He wanted it. He was ready.

"In hell everyone will have self-will, and therefore in hell is every kind of wretchedness and misery."

- Meister Eckhart

A WORD FROM THE AUTHOR &
ACKNOWLEDGEMENTS

Some stories incubate for a long time before finally revealing themselves. Others spring forth almost fully formed. This story was a combination of those two things. It sat, lurking in the back of my mind for many years, and then – nearly overnight, it seemed – it was complete.

Dark and Broken Things began life as a very simple idea: I wanted to retell *A Christmas Carol*, set in the modern day with a young but successful protagonist, and I wanted it to occur over the space of a few days while he is trapped in a hospital recuperating from a car wreck. Don't go looking *too* hard for the shreds of Dickens' venerable classic in the pages of this book, however, as very few hints of that concept remain in the end. The kernel of the idea was the thing. Something about it spoke to me, and so I kept it on the backburner. It tried very hard to become a story many times, but to no avail. The lead character kept morphing and the point of view kept shifting. But it just never felt *right*. And it never felt *real* to me.

Nothing much happened with the idea until my good friend and colleague, Linda Larsen, talked to me one day about her irrational fear of wheelchairs. The idea fascinated me and I thought it, too, might make a good story. But it was only once I *connected* it to my *A Christmas Carol* idea that everything began to click in my mind. During the course of one evening back in June of 2013, *Dark and Broken Things* went from being a nebulous but well intentioned story idea to being an actual tangible thing, something I could put my hands around. Suddenly, I knew the characters. David Daniel Grace became a man and ceased being a concept. I knew his life, his story, his arrogance, his pain. That one lynchpin idea, when connected to another long gestating idea, allowed the entire story of *Dark and Broken Things* to reveal itself to me. And I simply began writing at that point, more a stenographer than an architect, anxious to record the details.

I know as I write this – at a point in time before *Dark and Broken Things* has been released – that there will be some who will not be completely satisfied by the ending. I'm okay with that. There have been many stories like that for me, stories that I've read that left me somewhat cold or confused upon completion, stories I liked but didn't know why. Often those stories become my favorites in the long term. One example of this is *Lord of the Flies* by William Golding. The end felt like a cop-out upon first read and I was left unsatisfied, expecting so much more. It was only upon further reflection that I realized the story I thought I was reading – and thus, the ending I was expecting – wasn't the one the author was interested in writing. Another example, in film this time, was *Fight Club* by David Fincher, based on the book by Chuck Palahniuk. I walked out of the theater gritting my teeth, swearing at the ground, frustrated and let down by the ending, an ending I felt didn't live up to the rest of the film. Now, years later, I've seen that film dozens of times and count it among my absolute favorites, and I wouldn't change a thing. Please know, I don't intend to rank myself next to any of the above-mentioned visionary talents, by any stretch. I only ask that if you are of the "like it, but don't get it" crowd, that you give it time, let it simmer.

One thing I can assure you is this: there was no cheating. The end destination never wavered, even while the specific pathway I took to arrive there did. David's journey stayed on course. And the road is littered with breadcrumbs for those crazy enough to go and gather them up.

With that being said, I'd like to acknowledge and thank a few people who helped shepherd this book into existence. First, I'd like to thank my developmental editor, Naz Keynejad, who brought her unique perspective to the book. I talked about shelving the book or putting it in a drawer for awhile, and Naz talked me out of that. I'd also like to thank Linda Daft Larsen and Terrie Mathis for taking on the copy editing duties. I'm appreciative of the unique perspective you both bring. You take sandpaper to the rough edges and make something that's ready to view. As always, I take full responsibility if anything was missed. I'd also like to the thank the readers who participated in the focus group; your feedback was invaluable. I'd like to acknowledge the friends and readers who contributed to the Kickstarter campaign for the book, including Diane Langdon, Dori Kenworthy, Taylor Dorris, Mike Adams, Thomas Barragan, Pat Bearden, Denise Hughes, Janna Wilson, Stephanie Ayling Thompson, Mary Cancilla, Holly Stull, Erik Dutson, Rob Prentice, Ilene Haber, Colleen Devaney & Don Dyke, Michael L. Foster, Daphne Healy, Donette Spring, Jeff Farnham, Tammy Porter, Andrew McInally, Naz Keynejad, ErinnMolly Stock, Darin & Kathy White, Julie Pelton, Mary Mulhall, Kevin Mulhall, Wendy Cherry, Blayne Alexander, NitroJill and Dar, Tina Muraski, Monica Duvernay, Christa DiGeralamo, Mechelle Lee, Debi Pearson, Sean Wolpin, Heather Wynalda, Megan Taylor, Shelby Jones & Mark Miller, Sara Quick, John Muraski, and Donna, an avid fan. And, of course, Linda once again, for inspiring me, perhaps unwittingly, and then helping to brainstorm with me in the early stages. This book will always bear your DNA.

As usual, I'd also like to thank the team at Mothership Creative for working on all of my marketing elements; in particular, I'd like to acknowledge Charlissa Mann for managing the particulars, and Rick Simonton for overseeing the website and other graphic design efforts. And I'd be remiss if I didn't acknowledge the beautiful and haunting cover art, courtesy of Scott Zambelli, the internal layout by Natalie DeSavia, and the striking logo and cover design elements created by Grant England.

And, of course, as always, thank *you*. Ultimately I'm pleased with *Dark and Broken Things*. It is a story that has become deeply personal to me. David Grace is frustrating and stubborn and very hard to love sometimes, just as any of us can be. He is a mirror for me, the person I might have become had things gone a touch differently. I respect David's journey. But that means very little if there's no audience, no reader to take that trip alongside me, alongside David. Thank you for picking up this book and coming along for the ride. I hope you enjoyed it.

The journey matters.

- John Mulhall, November, 2014

AFTERWARD: LIFE AND DEATH IN
DARK AND BROKEN THINGS
by Wendy Cherry, Psy.D. Licensed Clinical Psychologist

I believe great books stay in your thoughts long after you finish them, motivating you to figure out why they have affected you so powerfully. *Dark and Broken Things* is a book that stayed with me. I loved this book. The end surprised me and actually moved me to tears. It led me on a thoughtful journey of pinpointing exactly why I had such an intense reaction to the story of David Grace.

I have my own ideas of what created someone like David, and many others who have found their need to love tied to pain, envelopment, rejection, or betrayal. Biology, psychology, and neuroscience have determined that we are hard-wired to connect to other human beings. The quality of our primary relationship determines how well we are able to connect to ourselves and others, and trauma can adversely affect this ability. To let go of our desire to connect, to love and be loved, can be a direct path to madness. Basic mistrust in others – an extension of not trusting ourselves – can create the illusion of demons and darkness underneath the mask of humanity. For David, not having anywhere to put his own childhood anger, fear, pain, and guilt forced him to adapt to his environment and lock his heart away. This adaptive strategy is not unusual, particularly in this day and age. We are currently living in a "left-brained" society, where focus on individual achievement, self-sufficiency, power, and material success has superseded our innate need to connect to others. All of us are immersed in this day-to-day struggle, and it is too easy to forget what actually makes our existence meaningful.

255

Existentialism puts forth that death gives meaning to life. When we think about death, most of us do not want to die badly. Personally, I hope to pass peacefully in my warm bed, with no warning or knowledge of the actual event. As a clinical psychologist, I strive to understand how people feel about death. Though some wish for it, and others fear it, a common thread is the notion of at least finally being at peace. *Dark and Broken Things* tests this notion. What if the way we live is connected to what we face when we die? We then have to consider the terrifying possibility that there is no peace to be found in death, unless we are able to find some semblance of it in life.

I found myself wondering why I love to read paranormal, horror, sci-fi, and fantasy. The answer has much to do with my work as a clinical psychologist. These books are an escape and provide an outlet from thinking about the very real things that truly frighten me. I realize that I will have to read *Dark and Broken Things* again, and probably a third time, in order to clearly see all of its metaphors and nuances. Much more than a supernatural thriller, it cleverly delivers a powerful message about how we live, how we die, and how these journeys may be tied together.

Bringing meaning to our lives is a timeless struggle for humanity, no matter how many times we witness the revelation that the answer lies in actually being human. The demons we create in a bruised mind and heart are much more terrifying than any paranormal creature, monster, or ghost. It is not dying that is the ultimate tragedy, but what we allow to die inside of us while we still live. Perhaps Charles Dickens said it best in his timeless classic, *A Christmas Carol*: "No space of regret can make amends for one life's opportunity misused."

www.ingramcontent.com/pod-product-compliance
Lightning Source LLC
Chambersburg PA
CBHW022036240626
47154CB00007B/2427